MW01173369

IN DEATH SURVIVE

ALSO BY ANDREW M. SEDDON

Stories of the Supernatural

Tales from the Brackenwood Ghost Club

What Darkness Remains: 13 Tales of the Supernatural and Unknown

Science Fiction

Red Planet Rising

Iron Scepter

Ring of Time

The Deathcats of Asa'ican and Other Tales of a Space-Vet

Wreaths of Empire

Historical Fiction

Imperial Legions

Saints Alive! Saints of Empire

Saints Alive! Celtic Paths

Non-fiction

Walking with the Celtic Saints

IN DEATH SURVIVE

ANDREW M. SEDDON

FAR
WANDERINGS

2018

FAR WANDERINGS

Copyright © 2017 Andrew M. Seddon

All rights reserved.

Cover illustration by Paul Drippé

Design by Lisa A. Nicholas of Mitey Editing (miteyediting.com)

The following stories have been previously published, and revised for this edition:

"The Ghost Dog of Stockton Bridge," *Thema*, Summer 2016, Vol.28 No.2, p. 95–106

"Dead Men Rise," *Legends of Sleepy Hollow*, David Neilsen, ed., Neilsen Books, 2015, p. 80–101.

"*In Solitudine, Mors*," *Twists of Romance*, ebShop, 2017.

... and in death survive
Through ghostly night.

"Roisin Dubh,"
Aubrey de Vere (1814–1902)

Dedication

For Mom and Dad—
for all you've done, and still do.

Acknowledgments

Thanks to Werner Lind and Colleen Drippé for comments and critiques. To David Neilsen for making *Dead Men Rise* a better story. To Lisa Nicholas of Mitey Editing for design and editing. To Paul Drippé for the painting that inspired "The Priory."

And as always, to Olivia, my much better half.

Author's Note

Readers of my previous volume of supernatural stories, *What Darkness Remains*, will notice a similarity between "The Power of the Dog" in that volume, and "Hunter's Moon" in this one. They are indeed two versions of the same story, but I hope that does not detract from any enjoyment received from them.

Father Vincent O'Gorman was indeed the priest at St. Edmund King and Martyr in Bury St. Edmunds during World War One, as mentioned in the story "*In Solitudine, Mors.*" I hope he doesn't mind the use I have made of him in the story.

About the Cover

I was gratified to receive the painting, "Church Ghosts" by Paul Drippé, that adorns the cover. I felt that it deserved to form the basis of a story, and so "The Priory" was born out of my interpretation of the painting's meaning. After the story was written, I asked Paul what he intended by the painting. He replied, "I had envisioned religious, who for whatever reasons, left the Church and now they are on a pilgrimage to return—only to find the Church devastated. They find now no reference to transcendent beauty, no statues, no altar, only a wretched table. My painting, "Church Ghosts," was inspired by German artist Caspar David Friedrich and his painting "Abbey in the Oakwoods", circa 1810. I found this prophetic, since some of his paintings were destroyed in the world wars and I can picture some of the churches bombed out in those same wars, the trees hit by shrapnel."

.

Contents

ONE

The Ghost-Dog of Stockton Bridge

"I ONLY HAVE ONE ROOM AVAILABLE," SAID THE female member of the couple standing behind the reception desk of the bed and breakfast, quaintly named "The Josephine." She ran her index finger down a ledger book, stopping at a blank line. "But I shouldn't let you have it."

"Why not?" I asked.

"It's haunted," she said apologetically. She was about fifty, slender, wearing a floral-patterned dress.

"Haunted?" I echoed, frowning, at the same time her husband, his weatherworn plaid shirt stretched over a beer-belly into jeans, said "Janet!" in an annoyed tone.

"Well it's true," she rejoined, an edge in her voice. "The gentleman"—she peered over the top of her horn-rimmed glasses at my business card—"Mr. Hayes has a right to know."

"It's bad for business," he argued. "You shouldn't be telling people nonsense."

"Haunted?" I asked again.

Giving her husband a final glare, she returned her attention to me and nodded. "Some people have left in the middle of the night. One woman was so hysterical we had to call the doctor. Ran into the street in her nightgown, screaming to wake the dead."

"Not to mention the mayor!" her husband growled. "All of them neurotic—"

"That's enough, Frank," Janet retorted. "They were perfectly ordinary people."

She smiled at me. "Of course, some folks don't mind a ghost.

Occasionally, people even ask for them. Ghost hunters, you know. I recall one—a retired librarian—nice lady—"

"Is it a horrible ghost, then?" I queried, visualizing terrified guests, and wondering if perhaps I would be better off moseying on.

"There is no ghost!" Frank exclaimed.

Janet leaned forwards. "It's a dog," she whispered.

My throat tightened.

"Crackpots," Frank huffed, "the whole kit and caboodle."

"Go away, Frank," Janet ordered. Frank raised his hands in mock surrender and shambled off.

Janet adjusted her glasses. "So, there we are. The Country Inn over in Riverton might have a room, although they're usually full on a Friday. It's about half an hour away. I'll call them for you if you like."

I thought for a moment, turning to look out the curtained window as I did. I'd taken the turnoff to Stockton Bridge on a whim, thinking that perhaps it might be a good place to spend the night.

Situated on a scenic byway rather than a main road, Stockton Bridge was a quaint New England town that had resisted being over-run by tourism and, in consequence, had retained its charm. Colonial-style buildings lined a few maple-shaded streets. A white clapboard church smiled serenely across a well-trimmed village green at the sturdy Town Hall opposite. A grocery, funeral home, post office, café, and several specialty shops completed the ensemble. And, of course, just outside the town's environs was the red covered bridge from which Stockton Bridge drew its name.

I was happy to have chanced upon this peaceful relic of a bygone era. It was one that could have graced postcards and calendars —and probably did.

Disliking the blandness of urban motels, I was pleased to

have discovered this guest house as well, which the waitress at the café had pointed out to me after I'd enjoyed a filling dinner of pot roast and apple pie.

The Josephine was a three-story house painted light yellow and adorned with chimneys, gables, and a large covered porch that ran around three sides. Gauzy curtains peeked through the partially open windows, and a cherry tree in full bloom graced the front yard.

It had appeared so inviting—much more so than a motel in bustling Riverton.

Not that I slept well anywhere, not for years. Not since—

Best not to think about that.

"A dog, you said?" I asked cautiously.

She nodded. "I haven't seen it myself, mind you."

It was getting late, I was tired, and I didn't fancy driving along narrow, winding roads in the dark.

I made up my mind.

"I'll chance the ghost," I said. "Let me have the room."

"Are you sure?" she said, raising plucked eyebrows. "I wouldn't want you to be disappointed."

"Perfectly," I said, removing a credit card from my wallet. "But I want the whole story."

"All right," she agreed, curving her thickly glossed lips into a slight smile. "But let me show you the room first, just to be certain you really like it."

THE ROOM TO WHICH Janet Wells conducted me was on the second floor, in a corner of the house. Facing me as I walked in was a four-poster bed with a scarlet canopy and more pillows than I could ever use. Behind the bed, a window framed the cherry tree. To my left, French doors opened onto a small balcony, and an oak chest of drawers supporting a Tiffany lamp was tucked into the corner. To my right, a door opened into a bathroom with a claw-footed tub. Just beyond that, a fire was laid but not lit in a stone fireplace. A bedside table was laden with a tray of biscuits and bottled water. The hardwood floor was spotless and shiny.

"It's perfect," I said, setting down my traveling case and perching myself on the side of the bed. "Now for the story. I suppose a town as old as this must have many ghosts."

She looked conspiratorial. "This house was built in 1802," she said, settling into a side-chair, "and you'd think so. But the truth is, our ghost is a mere five years old."

"A newcomer, eh?"

"Not everyone believes it."

"Like your husband."

She half-smiled. "Frank wouldn't believe it if it was five hundred years old."

"Do continue."

"Let's go back a few years," Mrs. Wells said. "The house was owned by an elderly couple, the Phillips. They were blind. He got around with a cane, while she had a guide dog. They didn't venture out much, but I saw them in church nearly every Sunday."

She motioned with her hand in the direction of the white church on the green.

"The dog, I'm sorry to say, looked most miserable."

"German Shepherd?" I asked, having seen photos of seeing-eye dogs, but she shook her head.

"A black Lab. Now, I never saw her hit it, mind you, but she treated that dog like a slave. Never a pat on the head or a word of kindness. It trudged along with its tail hanging and its head down as if there wasn't so much as a flicker of happiness in its life."

"That's not right," I said.

"It wasn't," she agreed.

"Back home I know a veteran who lost his sight in an

explosion in Iraq," I said. "He has a German Shepherd. He loves that dog, and the dog loves him right back. That dog knows he's doing a job and doing it well. Ears erect, head up—you can tell he's proud of what he's doing. Those two are partners—comrades—needing each other, looking out for each other."

"That's not how it was with Wanda Phillips," Janet said. "There was no love for that dog. It was just a thing—like his cane."

"What was his name?" I wondered.

"I don't know. She never said—would never tell anyone the dog's name."

"Peculiar."

"Controlling," she corrected.

We sat in silence for a minute. Then she said, "One day, Wanda Phillips came to church without the dog."

"What happened?"

"We wondered that too. All she would say was that something horrible had happened." She sighed. "If a dog could commit suicide, I wouldn't have been surprised if it did so. But maybe it ate something bad, was hit by a car, fell into the well and drowned, was stolen . . . ? Who knows?"

She rose to her feet. "The Phillips were carried off in a flu epidemic not three months after the dog disappeared. Frank and I purchased this house from their estate. This was their bedroom. The dog slept over there"—she pointed to a spot beside the fireplace—"on a threadbare mat hardly thicker than a sheet of newspaper."

She turned to leave. "And they always slept with the light on."

"Whatever for?" I asked, wondering what use light was to blind people.

"So any would-be intruder would know there was someone at home," she said.

"But surely the dog couldn't get any sleep!"

"She didn't care. Said it was her room and she'd do what she wanted."

"Abominable," I said.

"Do you have a dog?" Janet asked.

I looked down. "I did, until a few months ago. Molly died of cancer."

"I'm sorry."

"She was the most loveable mutt. Some days, I still can't believe she's gone. I've thought about getting another one—but I can't. Not yet."

"There are plenty of needy dogs," Janet said. "The shelters are chock full of them."

"I know. But with my new position—I'm on the road all the time—I just can't give a dog the attention it deserves."

"Maybe one day," she said.

"Maybe," I replied.

She paused with her hand on the doorknob. "Are you sure you'll be all right?"

"I'll be fine," I said, more confidently than I felt.

"Good." And then she slipped out the door, before I could remind her that she hadn't said a word about the ghost, just left me to assume . . .

IT WAS A cloudless night, with the moon shining silver above the cherry tree and sending shafts of light in through the window behind the bed. The old house had a cozy feel as its roof and beams crackled away the day's warmth. I hadn't heard a car drive by in hours.

I stayed up late reading, as I always did, and made great inroads into the biscuits.

I left the blind open when at last I finished my book, turned off the light and sank into the feather-soft mattress.

But despite the comfort, my sleep was light, as it inevitably was, my senses alert for the slightest sound . . .

The sound of something . . . approaching stealthily through the night . . .

If only Molly was still with me . . .

Molly had been my nocturnal salvation. I'd always slept well with Molly by my side.

But since I'd lost her, the night had become something to fear.

What was that?

I sat bolt upright, straining to hear.

Then it came again—a creak as of a door opening.

Bright moonlight was flooding the room with a milky radiance. I could see the three doors—to the balcony, the bathroom, and the hallway—quite clearly.

They were shut.

I lay back down. The house settling, that was all.

Then there came a clicking, as of nails on the polished hardwood floor.

Click, click, click, click, approaching the bed.

My heart pounded, and immediately I was transported to childhood. When I was eight or nine years old, I'd played hooky from school and gone to the zoo, sneaking past the ticket collector at the entrance. It was a large place, threaded by miles of winding trails between the exhibits. Sometime late in the afternoon, I became tired and lay down for a nap. When I awoke, it was pitch dark. The zoo had closed, and no one had noticed a small boy sleeping under a tree.

I knew immediately that I was trapped. The zoo was surrounded by a high chain-link fence sunk deep into the ground and topped with barbed wire. I could neither climb it nor crawl underneath it. I would have to spend the night lost in the zoo.

Accepting my fate, I hunkered down under the tree with my

arms wrapped around my legs, my heart racing like that of a gazelle pursued by a cheetah, my young mind conjuring dire fantasies.

What if the lions or tigers escaped? What if some hungry beast even now was creeping through the underbrush towards me?

In the distance, the wolves howled.

I shivered and made myself as small as possible.

I thought the night would never end—every rustling made me jerk awake, every slight noise broke me out in a renewed torrent of sweat. It was an eternity of terror, much worse than the thrashing my father gave me in the morning.

Now, I raised myself on an elbow, wondering what I might see.

Nothing.

Nothing but shadows cast by moonlight on the floor.

Click, click, click, click, coming closer to my side of the bed.

They paused, replaced by a soft panting.

I held my breath, conscious that I had broken out in goosebumps.

A human ghost I might have dealt with. But not an animal. Not an animal that might have dread designs on me . . .

You're thirty-two, I told myself sternly. Not eight.

Click, click, click, click, heading towards the fireplace, hesitating, then continuing to the other side of the bed.

Another pause. Then click, click, click, click, coming back towards my side, halting and panting.

I'd never gone back to the zoo—never gone to any zoo, since. I'd avoided animals for years. Even dogs, man's best friend.

That was, until Mollie came along. Dear, sweet Mollie, who'd captured my heart and made me laugh . . . brought me comfort in the night, banished the nightmares . . .

I peered into the moonlit room, wondering if the better

night vision that other species enjoyed would have helped me. I didn't think so.

Still nothing.

Once again, the clicks returned to the fireplace and the other side of the bed, then retraced their way to me again.

A third time the cycle repeated itself, as if whatever was making the noises was restless, undecided what it wanted to do.

I could well imagine a person of nervous temperament being driven to near-panic by the repetitive click, click, click of something unseen pacing around the room. I was close to it myself. I sent up a brief prayer addressed to Saint Francis, thinking he might be a good choice.

But then, I reminded myself, this wasn't a wolf, or a lion, or some other ravening beast. It was a dog ... man's best friend. A seeing-eye dog, trained to help people.

A dog that had been unappreciated, unloved ...

Strangely, as I thought that, my fear abated. And I detected something else in the restlessness.

Still half-raised—and surprising myself—I patted the bed. "Come here."

The clicking stopped, and I wondered if I shouldn't have spoken.

Then it resumed, once more heading around the foot of the bed.

I patted the sheets again. "Come here."

The clicks continued to the other side of the bed.

A third time I patted, then said, "It's all right."

The bed shook as if a weight had landed on it, bounced gently, then shook again as the weight flopped beside me.

The moon was bright. Something was indenting the sheets—something that I couldn't see.

I lay back down, conscious of a heaviness on my left shoulder, as if a muzzle was lying on it. I fancied that I felt a touch of breath ...

Mollie had lain against me like that.

But Mollie was dead—never to sleep beside me again—and oh, how I missed her ...

I reached behind me with my free hand to pull down the shade.

The room descended into darkness.

I draped my arm over a body that wasn't there.

And I fell asleep.

"DID YOU SLEEP well?" Janet Wells asked when I showed up in the breakfast room the next morning, having slept in late. A young couple was just departing, so I had it to myself, except for an elderly man who sat in a nook by the bay window, absorbed in his newspaper. She sounded curious.

"Very well," I replied. "Better than I have in a long time." I was, in fact, feeling incredibly rested and content.

"Then you weren't disturbed by the ghost?" she asked, pouring my coffee.

"Not at all," I answered. "In fact, we had a wonderful time together."

She almost spilled the coffee but made a valiant effort to avert disaster. "You did?" she squeaked.

"Most enjoyable. A delightful companion."

"Are you serious?" She turned to observe her husband who had just entered carrying a rack of toast. I suppose I sounded as if I had suddenly gone mad.

"Perfectly," I asserted.

"If you say so," she said doubtfully, making an effort to pull herself together, as Frank set the toast down on the table.

"My route will be bringing me near Stockton Bridge quite frequently," I said. "If I give you the dates, will you reserve that particular room for me?"

Her smile didn't seem quite natural—almost sickly. "That won't be a problem."

"Good," I said, spreading mixed-fruit jam on a piece of toast.

She headed back to the kitchen, followed by Frank.

"How very strange," I heard her say, just before the door closed.

And his reply: "You and your stupid ghost stories. It's a wonder we ever make any money on that room."

TWO

Ravensford

"I'M A MATERIALIST, THROUGH AND THROUGH," James Winston said, setting his bottle of Irn-Bru soda down on the table and wiping his lips, "and will be until the day I die." His blue eyes stared at his two companions as if daring them to contradict him.

"So, I suppose you don't believe in ghosts," Phillip commented, nonchalantly splashing malt vinegar over his fish and chips. He speared one of the latter with a wooden fork.

"Nope." James' shaggy blond hair bounced as he shook his head vigorously.

"Or haunted houses?" Megan added, intercepting Phillip's chip on its way to his mouth and popping it into her own.

"Nothing supernatural whatsoever," James replied firmly.

Phillip and Megan exchanged glances. The three sat at one of the handful of plastic-topped tables inside the chippie, having arrived before the shops on the high street closed for the day. Only a few customers were trickling in.

"Look," James continued, digging into his own chips, "where's the proof? Myriads of anecdotes, a few blurry photographs, and not a shred of anything even remotely conclusive. If ghosts are real, be they incorporeal beings, remnants of psychic energy, or whatever the current fashionable hypothesis happens to be, then show me where they fit on the electromagnetic spectrum."

"We're journalists, not physicists," Megan said, spooning into her mushy peas.

"But if we were to tell you about a haunted house not far from here . . ." Phillip prompted.

James grinned, baring a row of even teeth. "So that's it, is it? Going to issue a challenge, are you? Want the materialist to put his money where his mouth is?"

"Nothing so drastic," Megan said, laying a hand on his arm. "But we heard about this place, and it sounded interesting, and we thought who better than somebody with scientific training to investigate . . ."

"Too afraid to go yourselves, eh?" He bit into a sausage roll. "Worried by wind in the chimney or creaking doors? Scared of the thought of blobs of ectoplasm dripping from the ceilings? Petrified by moans and groans coming from the cellars?"

"This place does have a creepy history," Phillip said. "According to our research, the locals won't go near it, even in daytime."

"They never do," James chuckled. "All right, I'm game. Tell me about this place."

At the sound of a throat being cleared, the three looked up to find an elderly man in black clerical garb regarding them with a serious expression on his face. He was white-haired and stooped, and wore black clerical garb.

"Father Carrick!" Megan exclaimed, half-rising. "We were just—"

"I couldn't help but overhear," the priest interrupted. His gaze fixed on James. "And if you were talking about the place I think you were, I would advise you, young man, not to go anywhere near it."

His focus shifted to Phillip and Megan. "And shame on you two for even suggesting it."

"We meant no harm," Phillip protested. "It was more of an intellectual exercise."

"A very dangerous exercise," the priest said.

"Don't tell me there's anything to this haunted house nonsense," James exclaimed. "Although I suppose a priest is obligated to believe in the supernatural."

"There are good reasons for that," Father Carrick said, scowling at the thinly-veiled insult.

"Not in my books."

"Then maybe you haven't read the right books," the priest said tartly. "Be that as it may, Ravensford is best left alone."

"Cod and chips, Father," called the server from behind the counter, holding up a package wrapped in newspaper.

The priest, white-haired and stooped, turned aside. "Mark my words," he said, raising a cautionary finger. "Keep away from that place."

James waited until the priest had left the shop before bursting into laughter.

"What's so funny?" Megan asked.

"All of you," James replied. "Trying to make everything sound serious. I bet you put that old duffer up to it. Who was he, anyway?"

"Father Carrick?" Phillip replied. "He's just a local priest. Been here since the Middle Ages, give or take a hundred years. Fancies himself as something of a local historian."

"A little bit dotty if you ask me," Megan whispered, and Phillip sniggered.

"Why don't you suggest he go and perform an exorcism, then?" James asked.

"He's not that dotty," Megan said.

Phillip crunched into his fish, swallowed, then said, "Maybe we shouldn't have mentioned anything. Just forget it."

"Well, you can't stop now that you've raised my curiosity," James said. "At least tell me the story of this house."

"I suppose that can't hurt," Phillip mused.

"It would spare me the trouble of looking it up for myself,"

James said. "If there's one thing I can't stand, it's being left hanging."

"Just say you won't go there," Megan said.

James picked up his sausage roll again. "I'm listening."

JAMES THOUGHT ABOUT what his friends—acquaintances, really, since he'd never learned their surname—had related to him, as he ambled along the narrow lane towards Ravensford the following morning, pen and notepad in his pocket and camera slung over his shoulder. An early mist had dissipated, and the sun peeked from behind red-tinted clouds. The forecast called for rain later in the day, but for now, the weather was just perfect for a stroll. And the lanes, once he had escaped the boundaries of the town, were delightful, lush and green. Not that he normally paid much attention to the beauties of nature—he was more likely to be found in his office working through some abstruse mathematical problem—but he realized that it was good for his body to get out every now and then.

The lane made a left turn, and James veered off along an overgrown track to his right, cursing softly to himself as he brushed against a growth of nettles. The track had obviously not been traversed in a long time. Ravensford, he'd deduced from the map he'd consulted, lay in a hollow, totally secluded from the road.

It had been abandoned for decades, Phillip had told him, and was now supposedly nothing but a roofless shell. At one time, it had presumably been a desirable and valuable property—why, then, had it been left to the ravages of wind and weather, mouse and insect?

It was here that the story became murky, according to Phillip, although James thought it merely typical—rumors of unholy rites, a decadent family tainted by madness, the disappearance of pets and local children, a final catastrophe, and the surviving family members fleeing the shambles.

"How very Gothic," James had said disparagingly.

Indeed, it began to feel Gothic as a patch of cloud covered the sun and the landscape ahead greyed, while the surrounding hills remained bathed in sunlight. He became aware that he was walking in silence, the birdsong that had accompanied him on the first part of the walk having disappeared. Perhaps his presence—since humans were undoubtedly rare interlopers here—had frightened them into silence.

He pressed on, the track becoming less and less distinct the farther he went. And the grass, so verdant in early summer, became browner. He frowned. The land must once have been farmed intensively, he guessed, until its nutrients had been depleted.

He circled the side of a hillside and received his first glimpse of Ravensford. He paused, studying the scene.

The property did, indeed, lie in a hollow, sheltered from the winds which gusted over the hills in winter. Downhill and directly in front of him lay a patch of marshy ground punctuated by reeds and rushes. The marshy area merged into a gloomy lake fringed on its farther shore by a handful of straggly trees.

The track on which he stood wound around the marsh and the lake, terminating beyond the trees. And there, perched on a small knoll, stood Ravensford. At this distance, he could make out nothing but a hint of walls, but, even so, he felt a wholly irrational shudder of apprehension.

It was, of course, nothing but a product of his imagination, fueled by the fanciful story Phillip and Megan had spun for him. He chided himself mentally for allowing himself to be disturbed by such spurious nonsense.

After the remnants of the Dagenfields had abandoned

Ravensford, disappearing to only God knew where, the house had remained vacant for some time. Eventually, the deed became forfeit to the government for non-payment of taxes, and hence passed into the hands of an estate agent.

"It was hardly surprising that no buyer could be found locally," Phillip had said. "If tales of the Dagenfields' doings weren't enough, passersby reported seeing strange lights and hearing weird noises from the empty house. Shepherds claimed their sheep wouldn't venture near it. So, when finally an interested party arrived, it was a businessman from London searching for a holiday home."

As Phillip told it, the businessman returned from a remarkably brief inspection of the property with his face as white as chalk and had practically thrown the keys at the estate agent, swearing he wished he'd never set foot in the place.

"Probably one of those high-strung City types," James said with a yawn.

"Maybe," Phillip replied, "but when it happened again, a few months later, to a hard-bitten old spinster who collapsed and died of a heart attack at the top of the lane, people began to wonder."

"Old spinsters do that," James scoffed. "Even the toughest ones bite the dust sooner or later."

But word had spread, as it inevitably did, and interest in Ravensford, lukewarm to begin with, had cooled, nothing proceeding beyond half-hearted inquiries. As time passed, people who'd known the Dagenfields died off or moved away, and the legends about the family passed first into folklore, and then were mainly forgotten, as newer generations uninterested in the past arrived. And so Ravensford settled down to decades of slow decline, broken only intermittently by the odd event which sent reporters delving into the yellowing pages of old newspapers in search of copy, and briefly fanned

ANDREW M. SEDDON

the flames of sensationalism.

One such event was case of the transient found wandering in the vicinity with his mind gone—although, being a transient, he might have been mad to begin with. And there was the curious case of the shepherd who went in search of his missing sheepdog late one afternoon. He was last seen crossing a hillside in the direction of Ravensford. Neither he nor the sheepdog were ever seen again.

"Maybe he should have had a smarter dog," James had remarked dryly, thinking how a careless step could have landed the shepherd in a bog.

But now, as he drew towards the marsh, he wondered if he should have been so flippant. Because the place did seem to have a strange atmosphere—oppressive, almost threatening. It had, of course, to be due to the cloud-dimmed lighting and the dropping barometric pressure. Nothing supernatural there.

The marsh was stagnant, its oily waters exuding an odor of decay. Lime-green scum surrounded the bases of the reeds, and it required no effort of the imagination to picture himself, like the unfortunate shepherd, sinking into bottomless black ooze if he took a wrong step. He kept strictly to the track.

And then he reached the lake. Again, it might have been the lack of direct sunshine that plunged the lake into shades of charcoal grey. Perhaps in broad daylight it would shine blue, but somehow he didn't think so.

If the marsh had seemed sinister, the lake was positively malignant. Which was patently absurd. Natural features were neither good nor evil—they just were. Good and evil, he told himself, arose solely from the minds of men—social constructs devised to serve the needs of a culture.

As he studied the dark surface of the lake—a surface that gave him the impression that it would absorb the shadows of the trees, should they happen to fall in that direction—he noticed a vague disturbance: low ripples, a swirling as if something moved just beneath the surface. And yet the air was totally still—there wasn't so much as a breath of breeze to cause ripples.

Uncomfortable, he took a step backwards.

A few bubbles broke the surface of the lake. Marsh gas he supposed, perhaps disturbed by a fish. Fish. Of course. He gave a stilted laugh.

But the swirling seemed awfully large . . .

He hurried on, ascending a slight slope to the screen of trees. These, too, struck him as being abnormal, their leaves twisted and deformed. Some plant disease, obviously, or related to the depleted soil. Perhaps use of a now-banned pesticide.

It was no wonder that people avoided this place. One abnormality could be passed off, but a whole series of them . . . well, it took a stout—or a scientific—mind to place them in proper perspective.

He passed quickly between the trees, and there before him stood what remained of Ravensford. It must have been an impressive house in its time and, even in its ruined state, retained a certain grandeur. And yet it was a grandeur marred by something indefinable, as if something was slightly askew.

An intact portico shaded the entrance to a large central block from which two turreted wings protruded, imparting a castle-like appearance. In fact, it reminded him distinctly of Inveraray Castle, although on a more modest scale. But whereas Inveraray Castle gave the impression of Gothic solidity, Ravensford brooded—he could think of no better word—but brooded in what struck him as a baleful manner.

He could certainly understand why no one had ever purchased this property. Still, he reminded himself, there was nothing ghostly or supernatural about it—nothing that couldn't be explained by purely natural causes. Well, he would give the house a cursory examination, take some photos to prove he'd been here, and then return to tell Phillip and Megan that their stories were nothing but a load of rubbish.

He turned his steps to circle the house, which was of greater extent than he had initially realized. He made his way across a cracked and broken terrace, feeling weirdly as though the house was watching him from its barred, glassless windows. Strangely, he saw no evidence of other doorways.

His circumnavigation brought him to the main entrance, where once a pair of great wooden doors had hung. Nothing remained now but rusted hinges. He stepped inside.

As he had been led to expect, a large section of the roof had caved in, taking with it masses of the upper floors, leaving a debris-filled interior. The walls, though, made of stone, had defied the elements, and appeared remarkably thick—more so than one would normally expect.

Ahead of him, a great staircase rose to a landing, still partially intact, that spread to wings on either side. He saw no reason to explore more of the interior—what would be served by that?—but decided to climb the staircase to the landing.

As he did so, a few drops of rain struck him, and he looked up to see that the sky was now heavy with leaden clouds—the rain was arriving sooner than the forecasters had predicted. Reaching the top, he took a few photographs, then rested his hands against the bars of one of the vacant windows and looked out across a dreary landscape.

A ruined old house in a dismal location, that's all Ravensford was. Nothing more.

So much for the stories, and the admonition of the crazy old priest.

He would have the last laugh. Cool reason would triumph again.

And as he stood there, exulting in victory, he started when, from behind him—where he knew there was no door—came the sound of massive portals slamming shut and bolts being shot.

His mind said he should turn around as heavy footsteps plodded up the staircase behind him. But something primeval deep inside warned him it was better not to.

"DID YOU SEE the morning paper?" Phillip asked, indicating the pages spread before him on the breakfast table. Two days had passed since their conversation with the budding physicist.

"Not yet," Megan replied, pouring herself a cup of tea and blowing gently on it. "You've been hogging it."

Phillip took a bite of his toast and marmalade before answering. "There's a story here about a missing man. James Winston."

"Really?" Megan asked, with a slight elevation of her eyebrows.

"Apparently, he was last seen turning down the lane towards Ravensford by a postman making his rounds." Phillip rotated the paper towards her.

"Poor James," Megan said, studying a grainy photo of the missing man. "I feel rather sorry for him. He wasn't a bad sort."

Phillip Dagenfield reached across the table, took his twin sister's hand, and squeezed. "But on the bright side, Ravensford is satisfied. And that's what matters."

THREE

In a Churchyard Corner

I SAW HER IN A CORNER OF THE CHURCHYARD AS I was walking home from work, having stopped at a florist's on the way.

It was a pleasant autumn evening, and a playful breeze was tumbling the fallen leaves along the flagstones and whirling them around in miniature vortices. My route habitually took me past the church, but it wasn't often that I walked through the churchyard. Perhaps the dead reposing beneath haphazardly placed and often tilting headstones didn't mind, but I preferred to let them rest in peace.

Normally I skirted the moss-covered wall that separated the peace of the churchyard from the bustle of the outside world, but today I pushed open the wooden lychgate, and stood for a moment under its roof. Perhaps I had an premonition, for a shiver passed down my spine, and it seemed as if the frolicsome breeze declined to enter with me.

I wondered how many pall-bearers had rested their melancholy burdens where I paused now—for the world 'lych' meant 'corpse,' and it was here, in the Middle Ages, that the priest met the funeral procession to begin the burial rites. But there was no priest to meet me, only the ancient gray-stoned church standing in austere gravity across an expanse of immaculately trimmed grass.

I took a deep breath and followed the path, placing my feet gently, so as to make no noise.

It was as I reached the angle of the church that I spotted a figure seated on a bench beneath the shade of a spreading beech tree. My breath caught in my chest; attempting to ignore the hammering of my heart, I crossed the distance between us.

I sat down beside her, facing the comforting outline of the church with its stained-glass windows and Norman arches. At first, she seemed not to be aware of my presence. Her neck bowed, she could have been praying, with her gaze seemingly fixed at a point in the churchyard.

After a few minutes, she straightened, and I studied the profile that I knew so well.

Still, she didn't speak, and eventually I asked, my voice unsteady, "Why?"

"Because I was lonely," she replied softly, her voice hardly louder than that of a whisper. "So lonely. I couldn't take it anymore."

"I didn't know," I said. "Didn't realize—"

"I tried to tell you. You never listened. You were always too busy with something else. Work. Football. A novel . . ."

I hung my head. "It's true. God forgive me, I wish I had realized it sooner."

I longed to reach out and touch her hair.

The breath shuddered in my chest. "I loved you, you know," I said desperately. "The boys miss you. And so do I. If only we could go back—"

She shook her head. "It's too late."

I fell silent, thinking of what might have—could have—been, but for my blindness and stupidity.

She turned to look at me, and I saw compassion in her eyes.

"I harmed you, and offended God," I said. "Forgive me," I pleaded, my voice breaking, "even though what I did to you was unforgiveable."

She smiled and held up a slender hand. "My forgiveness is willingly granted, my dear. And don't despair," she added tenderly, surely knowing of my fear that my callousness had rendered us both beyond the pale of Divine forgiveness. "There is hope for both of us. Pray for me, as I shall pray for you."

"I will . . . for as long as I live . . ."

We sat in silence for a moment, as once we had years ago, when we were young and the days were long and fresh ahead of us.

All too soon, she said, "I must leave."

"Wait—" I began, reaching out, but, like the vanishing of a dream, she was gone.

With the sleeve of my shirt, I wiped the tears from my eyes, then rose. and laid the bouquet of flowers on her freshly-covered grave.

FOUR

In Solitudine, Mors

"YOU SHOULD GO AND STAY WITH YOUR COUSIN Clara," my mother said, in that tone of voice that indicted she'd already made up my mind for me. "Having a companion of her own age would be a great help to her."

"Is she not doing well?" I asked, looking up from the novel I was reading in my chair in the corner of the parlor.

"She says she's all right," my mother replied, handing me a letter, "but I don't think that's the case."

I nodded as I cast my eyes over the missive with its down-sloping handwriting. The sentences were innocuous—practically mundane in their content—but there was something about the tone and the physical formation of the words that spoke of deep unhappiness.

And why not? Six months ago, Clara had been the happiest of women, newly married to a charming and handsome man who was as deeply in love with her as she with him. How could she not be distressed that Jonathan, a talented musician and budding composer, had been sent by His Majesty to fight the Germans in the trenches of France, where the only music was the whine of bullets punctuated by the shrill whistle and deafening thunder of exploding artillery shells?

She had shared his last letter with us some six weeks ago when circumstances had brought us all to Ipswich, where we'd met for tea. In it, he had said that he was having a "jolly good time" with a company of "grand lads," but it was obvious that the sentiments were forced, designed only to attempt to reassure his wife.

"Certainly," I said to my mother. "I can catch the morning train to Bury."

"You'd best wire her first, so she'll be expecting you."

"Of course."

It didn't take me long to dispatch a telegram to Cousin Clara and pack a valise for the journey. A reply stating that she would be most pleased to have my company arrived that evening.

It was a pleasant morning as the train chugged through springtime countryside dotted with crocuses and daffodils. But my attention was held by the newspaper, with its accounts of the latest German offensive at Ypres and the endless list of casualties. My mind boggled at the thought of the thousands of men losing their lives every day, many suffering the most gruesome deaths. I counted myself fortunate that I was an only child, unmarried and unaffianced, whose father was too infirm, on account of a weak heart, to serve.

Clara was waiting for me on the platform at Bury St. Edmunds and greeted me with an embrace.

"It's good to see you, Meredith. Thank you for coming."

"The pleasure is mine," I replied, as we began to walk. The cottage that Clara and Jonathan had leased lay not far from the town center, just past the ruins of the old abbey.

I studied her covertly. Initially, I saw nothing amiss. Her golden hair was tied up neatly under a floral bonnet, and her gait was crisp. But touches of rouge could not completely conceal faint dark rings beneath her blue eyes or the red tip of her nose. The end of a handkerchief protruded from the cuff of her sleeve. Our conversation was of trivialities.

It wasn't until we were seated across from each other in her kitchen, with a pot of tea and plate of biscuits, that I was comfortable enough to ask her how she was doing.

Her smile was brave, but lacked conviction. "All right, I suppose."

"You must be very proud of Jonathan," I said.

"I am," she replied. "Very much so. I only wish that I could be there with him."

Clara was a petite girl; the thought was ludicrous. "It must be awful beyond words," I said. "I'm sure Jonathan would be horrified at the idea of you being in the trenches."

"But it seems so unfair." She motioned towards the window. "I will wake up to see the sun in the morning, while he . . . he may not." She refilled my teacup and set the pot down heavily. "If only I had been born a man!"

"Then you wouldn't be married to Jonathan," I pointed out, and she laughed.

I sipped my tea. "Have you heard from him lately?" I wondered.

She reached behind her and picked up a letter resting on a side table. "This arrived today."

"May I?"

She nodded and I unfolded the single sheet of paper that she handed me.

My darling Clara,

It has been a hard week. Do you remember Ben Foster? A Hun sniper did for him yesterday, poor chap. It is supposed to be spring, but you wouldn't know it except for the rain. At least Fritz is as wet as we are! In the breaks in the weather, we have been burying the dead as best we can.

Otherwise, I have been learning more card games than I knew existed—me, learning card games! I met a fellow from Bury, who has been telling me many curious stories about the town, which I shall have to relate to you one day.

Be a dear and send me some music paper, will you? Despite everything, melodies still enter my mind and I hate to waste them.

I do hope you are keeping well, and I hope to see you soon. Field Marshal French is certain the war will be over by summer. The Huns cannot last much longer.

Your affectionate husband,
Jonathan Wainwright

"He sounds reasonable, all things considered," I said.

"He's lonely," Clara replied. She sighed. "He's not a gregarious man . . . he doesn't make friends easily."

"You're lonely, too," I said.

"We're very much alike . . . we were meant for each other." She rose. "Have you had enough?"

"Plenty, thank you."

I helped her clean the dishes, and we passed the evening sitting beside the fire, I reading a novel and she writing a letter to Jonathan.

The following day was market day, and we spent an enjoyable morning purchasing the provisions for the coming week. To all appearances, it was a normal day as we walked among the stalls where townspeople sold eggs and cheese, onions and potatoes, bacon, chicken, fresh game—and yet we knew it wasn't. Too many of the lads were missing, and consequently the atmosphere lacked the gaiety that it would normally have possessed.

"Would you care to show me around the abbey ruins?" I asked after a light midday meal, thinking that the more I could get Clara out, the better.

"I don't know much of the local history—" she began to protest, before I interrupted.

"But you've lived here some months, while this is my first time in Bury."

"All right," she agreed, and we placed shawls over our shoulders and headed out.

"This was once one of the wealthiest Benedictine monasteries in England," she said as we passed through the gateway in the Norman tower into the abbey precincts, "until Henry VIII got his hands on it."

I sighed. So many religious houses had fallen into ruin after Henry promulgated the Dissolution in 1539. I suppose antiquarians and archaeologists appreciated remains more than myself, who would rather have seen the establishments intact and with their former glory. All that remained now, since the ruins had been used for centuries as a convenient quarry for building materials, were shapeless grass-covered mounds and piles of weed-choked rubble.

"King Edmund—perhaps I should call him St. Edmund— was killed by the Danes in 869 and was later buried here," Clara continued. "The abbey was built and enlarged over the centuries becoming one of the largest in the country, and a popular place for pilgrimages ..."

Obviously knowing more than she'd intimated, Clara prattled on, pointing out where the "Crankles," the fishpond near the River Lark, had been and informing me that there had been three breweries, as each monk was entitled to eight pints a day. She went into detail of the ups and downs of the abbey's history, conflicts between townspeople and not-always-Godly monks, until, fascinating as it was, names and dates became a blur, and I suggested that we return home for tea.

I PUT IT DOWN to fatigue, that first incident, although in retrospect I should not have done so. But hindsight, they say, is always perfect.

It was dusk, and Clara was making sure the windows were fastened, chatting idly as she did so, telling me about a neighbor who had offered her a little terrier to keep her company.

"You didn't accept?" I asked.

"I've never been fond of dogs, Meredith," she replied. "All the hair and the mess..."

"But still, don't you think—"

"I'm sure I could provide for its needs, but I couldn't give it much affection. So, what would be the point?"

We'd stepped outside the French doors for a breath of air and were facing across the lawn towards where the lane ran behind a low stone wall, when Clara gave a startled squeak.

"What is it?" I asked.

"There... just outside the gate... do you see...?"

"See what?"

She pointed. "There's a figure... a man..."

I peered in the indicated direction. "There's no one there."

"But there is!" Clara trembled.

"Nothing but a shadow from the willow," I said, putting my arm across her shoulder.

"But—"

"A shadow," I repeated firmly. "People imagine they see things in shadows all the time. Now come inside before you get a chill."

I shepherded her into the warmth of the cottage, looking back over my shoulder into the gathering dusk, but saw nothing out of the ordinary.

I made her sit down and take a nip of brandy to calm her nerves.

"But there was someone in the lane, Meredith, I'm certain of it," she insisted, and nothing I could say would dissuade her.

I THOUGHT Clara appeared distracted the following morning, as well as nervous. Her hand shook as she poured our morning cup of tea, and she had difficulty focusing on any task at hand.

We spent the morning at a ladies group knitting socks and

balaclavas to be sent to the boys in France and making chatty small-talk. I think we both found it tedious, although we felt good doing our small part to help the war effort.

In the afternoon, Clara wrote another long letter to Jonathan, which, as I learned, was her habit.

Her tension had dissipated by the afternoon, but towards evening it resurfaced.

"What's the matter, dear?" I inquired. "You seem jittery."

"Nothing," she replied, waving a slender hand. "Nothing at all."

I didn't believe her, and she knew it, but we said nothing more.

At dusk, though, after we had washed and put away the dishes, I found her standing outside the French doors.

"What are you looking at?" I asked.

"He's inside the gate," she replied. "Do you see?"

"Nothing," I said, feeling a twinge of worry.

She squinted. "I can't quite make him out . . ."

"Come inside and have a cup of Horlicks. It will help you sleep."

She followed me, unresisting.

"Jonathan liked his bedtime Horlicks," she said sadly. "I wonder if he gets it at the front."

"Undoubtedly," I said, trying to sound reassuring.

The next day, being Sunday, we went to Mass at St. Edmund King and Martyr Church, a Classical Revival building dating from 1837. I confess that my mind was rather more distracted than it should have been, and that day the disquietude was mine, as I wondered how Clara would fare come evening.

I tried to enjoy the stroll upon which she took me around the town, introducing me to such acquaintances as she had made.

"I do hope Jonathan is all right," one middle-aged woman told us. "I so miss hearing his voice on a Sunday."

"And I miss it every day," Clara said.

We stopped to admire a garden ablaze with larkspur, snapdragon, dog's tooth violet, and trillium.

"Have you ever been in love, Meredith?" Clara asked.

"No," I replied. "I have not been so blessed."

"It's wonderful and terrible at the same time," she said softly. "Sometimes I dream of Jonathan lying there dead in the mud, and wish that if only I could die with him . . ."

"Don't be morbid," I said, while thinking that her dream might be all-too-true.

We proceeded home in silence.

She seemed subdued for the remainder of the afternoon, and once again, come evening, she opened the French doors and ventured outside.

"Clara," I began, "you shouldn't—"

"He's there," she interrupted. "Just beside the willow."

The willow, I should mention, stood some yards inside the gate.

"There are only shadows," I said. "I'll prove it to you."

I strode briskly down the flagstone path until I reached the willow, then pivoted to face the house and spread my arms.

"See? No one here!"

To my amazement, Clara burst into sobs, covered her face with her hands, and dashed back into the house. I heard her footsteps going up the stairs.

I hurried after her and heard her crying in her bedroom.

"Clara! What's the matter? Open the door, dear."

But she didn't answer, and after a few minute I left her to her tears and sat by myself in the parlor.

CLARA DID NOT come down for breakfast on Monday, so I left a note on the table telling her that I was going into town by myself. There, I presented myself at the doctor's surgery and, by dint of insistence, secured a meeting with that worthy gentleman. I desired to speak to him about her privately, as I was afraid that suggesting she see him in person would ruin such confidence as she had in me.

He listened to me patiently as I explained the details of Clara's behavior, then sat quietly in thought for a moment, tapping his pen on the desk.

"I don't believe it's anything to worry about," he said at last. "I expect that she's suffering from a type of grief reaction. Melancholia. She's lonely."

"She is," I confirmed.

"The same type of thing can happen when a spouse dies, and the surviving spouse feels the presence of the departed one." He reached for his prescription pad, wrote quickly, tore off a sheet, and handed it to me.

"This is for a mild sedative. See if it helps her."

I left the doctor's office with my mind no more at ease than when I had gone in.

I sought out the parish priest, and Father Vincent O'Gorman was somewhat more reassuring. "In my short acquaintance with her I have found Clara to be a very sound-minded young woman," he told me, "but of a slightly nervous disposition, so I'm not surprised that she's expressing her anxieties in this— shall we say, unusual—form. It's better than having hysterics. And believe me, some of the young women in Bury have done just that... especially when the letter arrives."

He didn't have to explain what letter.

"But what can I do?" I asked.

"Pray for her," he said, "for both of them, as I will. And keep on being there for her. What she needs is a friend."

"She needs Jonathan," I corrected.

CLARA SEEMED calmer when we met for tea.

"Where did you go today?" she asked.

"To the library," I said, truthfully enough, as I had gone there to replenish my stack of novels.

"I can't read anymore," she said wistfully. "I just can't keep my concentration long enough."

She handed me a letter. "This came in today's post."

My darling Clara;

I have written you a Chanson d'Amour, although only in my head, as the music paper has not as yet arrived. I do hope that I shall have chance to write it down just in case—but let me not imagine that.

Fritz has been shelling us relentlessly the past few days—surely a prelude to an assault. We have taken some casualties, but new boys have arrived to take their place. One chap even knew my Uncle Felix—do you remember him? The one who played the clarinet so abominably? It is quite curious the people you meet.

I am well, aside from wet feet—it is still appallingly damp here. Be a good girl and send me some new socks, would you?

I wish we could walk by the Lark together . . . I am so sick of card games . . . I never liked them very much, as you know.

But I should not complain.

The chaplain, Fr. Frederick, has been most encouraging. He prays with the men daily and says Mass. He is as stout-hearted a fellow as can be imagined.

Well, I must go. The Colonel will be conducting an inspection later, and we must make everything as shiny as possible.

Affectionately,
Your Jonathan Wainwright

"I'm glad he can obtain spiritual comfort," I said.

Clara folded the letter and pressed it to her bosom. "If only I could see him. Really see him . . ."

IT WAS I WHO felt restless that afternoon, and also at something of a loss. I attempted to play the piano while Clara wrote a letter to Jonathan, but my heart wasn't in it and I made a dreadful hash of several Bach preludes. Clara was polite not to comment on my ineptitude.

I picked at my dinner so listlessly that Clara remarked upon it.

"I just don't know how to help you," I said.

She gave a short laugh and reached over to pat my hand. "Oh, Meredith, just having you here is a comfort. I can't tell you how much."

I was pleased by her appreciation and made an effort to enjoy the custard trifle she had made for dessert.

But my worries returned again as night was falling, and Clara, wrapped in her dressing gown, stepped outside.

"He's there," she said, as I came up behind her. "In the middle of the lawn."

"It's only a shaft of moonlight," I said.

"I know you think I'm going crazy," she replied, "but I'm not."

"Only the moonlight in the mist," I repeated, as something white swirled and dissipated.

The smile that she turned upon me was tender. "I can feel it," she said. "It won't be long now."

"What won't be long?" I asked, but she made no reply.

I stared at the moonlit lawn after she had gone back inside, but despite my best efforts could make out nothing. I shivered at the thought of something unseen coming closer and closer to the house each night . . .

And it puzzled me that Clara didn't seem to be afraid.

I DIDN'T SLEEP WELL that night. A sense of dread accompanied me through the nocturnal hours. I dreamed of something white and formless slowly but steadily approaching... my throat grew tight and my breath came in labored gasps as something reached out to brush my cheek—and I awoke with a start to find the curtain blowing across the head of the bed.

A stiff breeze was wrapping itself around the house and gusting in through the open window. Annoyed with myself for having left it open, I pulled down the window sash and tried vainly to go back to sleep.

I was surprised to find Clara in an almost excitable mood at breakfast.

"Let's go shopping, Meredith," she said, polishing off a plate of bacon, eggs, sausage, and black pudding.

"What for?" I asked groggily, downing another cup of tea in an attempt to wake up.

"A new dress," she replied, putting her dishes in the sink.

"The shops won't be open yet," I grumbled.

"Of course they will. It's almost ten!"

Ten? I'd been sitting over my tea for nearly an hour.

"You have plenty of dresses," I said, hoping to abort the shopping expedition. "Do you have any aspirin?"

"Do come," she said, handing me a bottle followed by my coat.

Together, we traipsed along the high street window-shopping, until a dressmaker's caught her attention. We went inside and a shop-girl approached and asked what we were looking for.

"Something pretty," Clara said. "More than that. Something elegant. Appealing."

"What's the occasion, ma'am?" the girl asked.

"Never mind that," Clara said, although I wanted to know as well.

The girl hurried away.

"It's for Jonathan," Clara whispered to me.

The news, as always, had been depressing, despite the transparent gloss put on even the worst setbacks.

"But Clara! The war may drag on for months... maybe years! It might be a long time before Jonathan comes home."

I didn't say *if he ever does*, although I thought it.

The look she gave me was mysterious—I didn't know how to interpret it, and I didn't inquire further as the shop-girl returned bearing an armload of dresses.

I'll give Clara credit for being decisive. She narrowed the list of possibilities quickly, and then went to the dressing room to try on one—just one—selection.

When she emerged, she looked stunning in a mid-calf-length dress of a pale bluish gray, embroidered at the neck and hems with a design of blue and white daisies. It was simple yet elegant.

"What do you think?" she asked.

"Jonathan will love it," I answered. "Just make sure to retain your figure."

She laughed prettily, and the purchase was made.

"Let's walk around the abbey again," she suggested after lunch. My headache had abated, and I acquiesced to her suggestion.

The nighttime wind had brought a covering of cloud that lingered through the day, yet it didn't feel like rain.

"Do you ever feel as if they are still here?" Clara inquired, as we ambled through the ruins.

"Who?" I asked.

"Why, those who used to live, and work, and pray here," she said, sounding surprised.

I shrugged. "I don't know. Sometimes, in church, perhaps..." Uncomfortable, I let the sentence drift off.

"I do," Clara said. "It's almost as if they were just around a corner. I wonder if we are ever truly alone, even though we might feel that way."

She perched on a pile of rubble and seemed lost in thought. Perhaps the separation was becoming too much for her. I didn't quite know what to say.

"I'm sure the saints can help us," I mumbled.

"Yes," she said quietly. "I ask them to aid Jonathan. Especially St. Martin of Tours and St. George. The patron saints of soldiers, you know."

She sprang to her feet, suddenly animated. "Let's go home, Meredith. I must do my hair and get ready."

"Ready for what?" I wanted to know, but she was already walking briskly away.

I DON'T QUITE know how to explain what happened after supper that day. Father O'Gorman appeared to understand when, later on, I talked to him in an attempt to ease my own mind. Otherwise, I told no one.

Clara spent hours bathing, brushing her hair, and fixing her make-up. She asked me to help her put on her new dress, which she complemented with matching sapphire earrings and necklace.

"You look wonderful," I said, "but won't you tell me what it's all about?"

"Jonathan gave me this necklace and earrings for our wedding," was her reply.

She sat at her dresser, gazing at a picture of her husband looking handsome in his uniform, his eyes kind, his features regular, and his mustache neatly clipped. I had to admit she had chosen well; they had been an attractive couple at their wedding, she slender and graceful, he dashing in a well-cut suit.

She seemed disinclined to speak further, and I left her to her reverie.

Not knowing what to do—should I contact the doctor or the priest about her again?—I draped a shawl over my shoulders and went out into the street.

If she was going mad—seeing strange figures at night, buying a new dress and getting gussied up for no reason—what, really, could anyone do for her? She would perish in an asylum.

I walked to the end of the block and turned around. The postman, making a late delivery, passed me, touching his cap in silent greeting.

I had nearly returned to the house when a cry pierced the night. I knew instantly that it was Clara.

In my mind I can hear it still—a cry the likes of which I had never heard before and have never heard since—a cry of utmost anguish mixed with indescribable joy.

I dashed inside, took the stairs two at a time, and burst into Clara's room. She was slumped forward over her writing desk, a post office telegram clutched in her hand. Only the first few words registered to my horrified eyes—

War Office, London … Deeply regret to inform you …

"Clara!" I gasped, feeling her neck for a pulse and finding none.

Something—I don't know what—prompted me in that awful moment to turn to the window. I parted the curtains and looked out. The moon was bathing the lawn in silvery light, and there, near the willow tree—

—two figures embraced. I saw them as plainly as if it had been broad daylight. One was a handsome man in military uniform, the other a woman in an elegant blue-gray dress, wearing a sapphire necklace.

They kissed, then, holding hands, turned towards the lane and together disappeared into the moonlit night.

FIVE

Dead Men Rise

THE RUSTY METAL OF THE OLD WROUGHT-IRON fence bit into my palms as I braced myself against the railings, afraid that my quivering legs would give way in—I glanced at the luminous dial of my watch—five minutes.

Beyond the railings, rows of crooked tombstones shone milky white in the pale light of a nearly full moon, while just over the rise the brooding bulk of Muhheakunnetuck Farm lay grim and forbidding.

Beside me, my cousin Russell shifted from one foot to another.

"Do you want to move closer?" he whispered.

"Are you nuts?" I whispered back, not moving my gaze from the ranks of grassy mounds.

"Maybe you're right," he said and edged a few feet further away.

How could so few minutes take so long to pass? I wished this to be over. Or did I? Another part of me wanted the moment never to arrive.

I took another glance at my watch.

Three minutes.

Inside the fence, close to one of the graves, stood another figure, his black clericals making him seem as if he were but one more of the shadows that crisscrossed the lonely hillside.

I heard the rustle of pages as he opened a book—I assumed it contained the burial office, or perhaps a rite for exorcism — and began to recite. Only the whisper of his elderly voice reached me, like the rattling of dead leaves.

My knuckles ached. I tried to relax my grasp, but my hands refused to obey my will. Perhaps the pain would help me keep my grip on sanity.

I could turn away. Leave this accursed place. Try to believe the words of the poet Swinburne, that "dead men rise up never."

But I couldn't and I wouldn't.

Father Connor was here because of me. I owed it to him to stay.

And I? I was here because of Russell.

No. I was here because I couldn't leave the past alone. Because I couldn't forget what I had seen before. Because "life has death for neighbor..."

Another glance. One minute.

My pulse pounded in my ears, drowning out Father Connor's raspy voice and the Latin words. For a moment, my vision grayed, and I forced myself to slow my panted breathing.

Dead men rise up never...

Dead men rise up never...

I repeated the words beneath my breath, as if that would somehow make them real.

A sudden intake of breath from Russell startled me, and then I saw it, at first no more than a faint haze as of thin mist emerging from the lumpy mound of the grave, but then like a slurry of congealed moonlight, twisting and writhing as it elongated into a bizarre parody of a human form...

I forgot the pain in my hands.

Forgot Swinburne's words.

Forgot everything.

Because, just as it had in my dream, the awful thing turned to face me—

ANDREW M. SEDDON

IT WAS ALL BECAUSE I had received, out of the blue, an invitation from my cousin Russell to be his guest at the rambling old farmhouse in the hills outside Sleepy Hollow that he had recently inherited from my Uncle Zachary. Thanks to a handful of visits during childhood, I remembered it with trepidation—a maze of oddly-shaped rooms and long corridors, of gloomy corners and twisting staircases, where a sudden creaking in the shadows paralyzed the lungs and the limbs with dread, in case something more than settling framework was lurking there...

I had feared those family visits to the ancestral home and the unsettling feelings I encountered there; even my youthful spirit knew that something wasn't right about Muhheakunnetuck Farm.

Although I was fond of Russell, I don't recall being particularly distressed when a falling out between my father and his brother had resulted in Dad uprooting our family from nearby White Plains to Asheville, North Carolina. Our two branches thus diverged, and so Cousin Russell's letter caught me by surprise. Contact with him over the years had been sporadic and typically limited to a card at Christmas and—if it entered either of our minds—one at birthdays. I knew that Russell had gone into law, specializing in divorce, and had made enough money to retire promptly upon receiving his inheritance. For this, I envied him.

He had never married, perhaps having been dissuaded by seeing the results of too many ill-advised unions. In this I had, unintentionally, emulated him.

My career path had landed me in northern Virginia, but at the time his letter reached me, having been forwarded by my house-sitter, I was working on a project involving the expansion of a hospital in Nassau County. A long weekend in Sleepy Hollow seemed the perfect antidote to the frustrations of dealing with obtuse administrators with grandiose ideas completely at odds with the necessities of reality—plush carpets in birthing rooms, I ask you!

Although Russell was a firm believer in the ancient art of hand-written letters—at least where family was concerned—in the interests of time, I emailed him a reply, received a positive response, and the following weekend took the train to Sleepy Hollow.

Russell met me at the station, a tall, angular man with short black hair, dancing blue eyes, and somewhat sunken features—the classic Bayard family trait, which suited him but had done me no good at all. He had a habit of repeating everything he said two or three times, which, for the sake of brevity, I shall not reproduce.

"Jenny!" he exclaimed, bounding across the platform. "What a pleasure!" He wrapped long arms around me and squeezed.

"It's good to see you again," I answered, extricating myself from the tight grip.

He picked up my overnight bag, slung it over his shoulder, and pointed. "Car's over this way."

"Is Sleepy Hollow really haunted?" I asked as we climbed into Russell's black BMW convertible—a cool 100K, I guessed—and headed through town. "I mean, aside from the Headless Horseman? Because I've had more than my fill of headless bureaucrats lately."

Russell laughed. "The poor guy's become a victim of commercialization. I wonder if he knows!"

I returned his laugh. "But seriously?"

"Well," he said, "there's the bronze lady in the cemetery. She's supposed to cry or haunt you if you kick her in the shins."

"Sounds painful."

"But if you mean ghosts . . . there are more of them than you can shake a stick at."

"Seriously?"

"Seriously. Dozens of them, between here and Tarrytown." He gave me a sideways glance. "I even have my own."

I started. "You?"

He nodded, deftly swerving around a texting teenager who had stepped into the road. "At least I think I might. The third Sunday of the month, that's when he appears."

"He who?"

His lips thinned. "Not at the moment. I'll tell you tomorrow night. For now, just enjoy the drive."

"Waiting drives me crazy," I said, but he paid no heed to my complaint.

I was annoyed, but I felt some of my tension ebbing away as the powerful car purred through the gently rolling countryside. I've always loved farm country, tree-lined roads, and deciduous forests. And May is a beautiful month.

Russell asked me about my work as an architect, my parents, my—non-existent—love life, and sundry relatives.

"I never really knew Uncle Zachary," I said.

"A bit of an odd duck, really," Russell said, "although I shouldn't speak ill of my own father. He wasn't a bad sort, all things considered, but I was glad to escape the paternal residence."

"But now you're back in it."

"But now it's mine." He turned the BMW into a curving drive. "And here it is."

The farmhouse, as I mentioned, was rambling, but that adjective hardly does it justice. The stone-built main building dated from the late 1700s, but subsequent generations had made innumerable modifications—another room here, a loft there, a passageway, a staircase—until it was a positive jumble of confusing twists and turns. It was, in short, an architectural nightmare.

But it was a nightmare that had been freshly painted, its chimneys and steps repaired, and its windows cleaned and gleaming. The lawn was trimmed, and new mulch surrounded flower beds.

"The old place looks better, doesn't it?" Russell said as I paused outside the heavy front door after he unlocked it.

That wasn't why I hesitated, but sensing that he desired approval, I said, "You've done wonders with it."

I took a deep breath as I stepped over the threshold.

Some old houses have an inviting air about them, but Muhheakunnetuck Farm—so called after the Iroquois name for the nearby Hudson River—wasn't one of them. It had a brooding air of senescence, as if a house—and I know this sounds strange—could have Alzheimer's disease. But it wasn't a benign senescence; rather, there was an ill-defined sense of malignancy, yet a malignancy that had faded into a shadow of its former self, like an evil that was no longer active but only dimly remembered.

I had sensed it in childhood without knowing what it was, but now I could put a name to it. It made my skin crawl.

Russell conducted me through newly redecorated rooms filled with antique furniture—he pointed out a beautiful inlaid Renaissance buffet and a gorgeous Burgundian grandfather clock with obvious pride—to a bedroom on the second story. "I only use part of the house," he said as we mounted the stairs, "but feel free to look around as much as you wish."

I had no desire to wander through that house. Something of what I perceived must have shown on my face.

"You feel something, don't you?" Russell asked.

I nodded. "Don't you?"

He shrugged. "I grew up in this house."

I shook my head. How he could not detect the weight that settled like the oppressive heaviness before a thunderstorm?

He settled himself on the four-poster bed in what was actually an attractive room furnished with a dresser, a chest, and an armchair. The wallpaper was new, as was the carpeting.

"Why did you want me to come?" I asked.

He glanced up, his expression serious. "Back when we were kids you always seemed so level-headed, so . . ."

"Boringly normal?"

His quick grin returned. "We come from a strange family, you and I. But the strangeness seems to have skipped you."

"Does this have anything to do with your ghost?" I wondered, not sure whether his last remark was intended as a compliment or not.

His gaze sharpened. "You were always quick-witted, Jen. Yes, it does."

"Then shouldn't you tell me—"

"First, I want to find out if you see what I do . . . or what I think I do."

"As long as you remember that I'm an architect, not a psychiatrist. I don't deal in visions or hallucinations."

He ran a hand along his brow. "I hope it's not a hallucination. I'd rather it were a ghost."

"How come I never heard about this supposed apparition before?"

Russell pursed his lips. "I don't believe our fathers ever spoke about it. Maybe it's just a goofy family legend. But I never saw it as a child . . . and that's why . . ." He broke off.

My chest constricted. "Look, Russell, I don't know that I'm the right person—"

He rose to his feet, interrupting me. "It's a lovely day. How about a walk? Work up an appetite for a Yankee pot roast."

"Suits me," I said.

Outside the house, the sense of gloom subsided and vanished completely as we strolled through an apple orchard alive with the hum of bees and the buzzing of insects. I needed to get out more, I told myself, inhaling deeply of the fresh air.

Muhheakunnetuck Farm was only a remnant of its former self, various parcels having been sold off over the centuries when a need for money arose. But a not-inconsiderable amount remained.

I asked Russell what he intended to do with it.

"Keep it as it is, I expect," he replied. "There's no need to sell it or develop it."

I was glad to hear him say that, as so much lovely country-side was succumbing to development—perhaps a strange thing for someone in my profession to admit.

On a low ridge, a wrought iron fence enclosed a square of land.

"The family cemetery," I said, walking over. "I'd forgotten it existed."

I paused, studying the rows of tombstones. Some remained vertical while others leaned at drunken angles; a few still presented shiny marble faces, while most were encrusted with lichen and showed the weathering of years. And as I gazed at them, a strange sensation, akin to what I had felt in the house, touched me like a cold, wet tendril creeping under my shirt and slithering up my lower back. I shivered.

"It's here, isn't it?" I asked softly.

Russell tried and failed to keep a flicker of surprise from crossing his face.

"Tomorrow night," he reiterated, the words sounding ominous, and led the way to a path that meandered through the woods.

THE POT ROAST, SERVED on floral-patterned Royal Doulton china, was delicious, and after dinner we relaxed in rocking chairs on the front porch, enjoying the cool evening breeze. Russell read a novel while I tried to focus on a crossword puzzle.

Later, he produced mugs of hot apple cider, before I retired to wallow in a huge claw-footed bathtub and work out the knots that had mysteriously formed in my upper back.

I was afraid that I wouldn't sleep well in the house, despite the feathery-soft bed, and I didn't. It wasn't just the trepidation as to what I might—or might not—see upon the morrow. Neither was it those childhood impressions resurrecting themselves from my subconscious and forcing themselves upon my adult mind.

It was as if the house didn't want me to sleep—as if it had aroused from its own troubled slumber and was regarding me with the decayed eyes of generations past, attempting to impress itself upon me... to seduce me, entice me, if necessary compel me...

To what?

I didn't know.

I'd never had much interest in my family history. I had no idea what had transpired in this house to create the aura of brooding malevolence.

Unable to stand the sense of scrutiny, I jumped out of bed, parted the curtains, and flung open the window. The soft touch of the nighttime breeze stroked my skin like the caress of a lover, while the moon flooded the hills with a gentle light. From this angle the cemetery wasn't visible, and for a moment, my fears abated.

But as I turned to return to bed, I wondered if I had made a mistake in accepting Russell's invitation.

"DID YOU SLEEP WELL?" Russell asked the next morning while laying out a hearty breakfast of bacon, eggs, sausage and hashbrowns.

"The bed was lovely," I replied, not wishing to admit to my nocturnal misgivings.

"Good." He sounded relieved. "I thought today I'd show you the sights. The Old Dutch Church, the Philipsburg Manor, the cemetery..."

"Love to," I said, "but take me into Sleepy Hollow for Mass, first."

"I forgot that you had gone Papist," he teased. "Not, of course, that you were the first."

"Only the first in our generation," I said.

Accordingly, he dropped me off outside St. Teresa's Church.

"I'm going to the country club to practice my putting," he said. "Be back in an hour."

Russell had always been punctual, and when I emerged from church an hour later, he was sitting on the hood of his car waiting for me.

We spent a pleasant day exploring the town, broken up by lunch at a tavern overlooking the Hudson River, and then dinner at a riverside eatery under the Tappan Zee Bridge.

"When do we need to be ready to see the ghost?" I asked as the sun disappeared and the rainbow of colors on the water of the river faded to gray.

"10:05," Russell said. "On the dot."

"I thought ghosts were unpredictable things—showing up whenever they wanted to, not bound by a clock."

Russell shrugged. "This one is punctuality... I was going to say 'embodied' but maybe 'disembodied' would be better."

I chuckled, more to hide my nervousness than from humor. "It will be a new experience for me."

We returned to the melancholy farmhouse, where, to pass the time, Russell regaled me with tales of Sleepy Hollow's other ghosts.

Eventually, he led me out onto the back porch, where we had an unobstructed view towards the ridge.

The moon, a few days shy of full, rose above the hills into a cloudless sky, casting pallid light across the fields and woods and illuminating the cemetery. The wind ghosted through the trees like something alive.

Russell checked his Rolex. "Almost time."

A thrill—or was it a chill?—tingled my nerves. I had never seen a ghost before, and I wasn't sure that I wanted to. Reading about them, or talking about them, was one thing; seeing one in the flesh—I grimaced—lack of flesh, rather—was quite another.

Maybe I wouldn't. Maybe Russell had been imagining things. He didn't seem crazy, but really, I hardly knew the man . . .

"Time," Russell said and I tensed, peering at the cemetery.

At first, I saw nothing. Then . . .

Something white, insubstantial, rose from the ground . . .

"Mist," I said, hating the shakiness of my voice.

"Watch," he said.

The mist elongated and—it couldn't, my mind was conjuring shapes out of nothing—assumed human form.

I gripped Russell's arm hard enough that he exclaimed.

The figure writhed and twisted, straining upwards, stretching and extending as if reaching for the oblivious moon, becoming increasingly distorted, like a character in one of El Greco's more bizarre paintings.

And yet it failed to break free, tethered to the ground by an invisible cord.

At this distance I couldn't see its face—if it even had one—and yet I had the impression of a grotesque visage, distorted by pain and frustration, yet unmistakably Bayard.

And as I stared in horror, the tormented form retracted,

losing its human likeness, as if being sucked back into the waiting earth.

Then it was gone.

My breath exhaled with a rush and I stood in silence for a moment, my legs quivery, my head swimming. A sudden cramp in my left hand reminded me that I was still clutching Russell's arm. Embarrassed, I let go, and reached for the porch rail instead.

"Flashlight," I said, forcing the word out.

"What?" Russell exclaimed.

"Flashlight," I repeated impatiently. "Have you got a flashlight?"

He slipped inside and returned with the requested object. I flicked it on and by its light made my way across the yard towards the cemetery, conscious of the hammering of my heart and glad for Russell following a few feet behind.

I paused for a second outside the wrought iron fence. What was I doing? This was the sort of thing that dumb people did in scary movies and paid the price for.

Except that this wasn't a low-budget horror flick. This was real.

I became conscious that Russell was watching me. I had to be the sensible, level-headed Jenny that he expected me to be. Plus, I didn't like mysteries. I didn't like the unexplained. I preferred my world to be all neat and tidy, like a finished architectural drawing.

I thrust my weight against the rusty gate. It yielded with an ear-piercing screech, and I crept in among the last resting place of the departed.

Which grave had the apparition appeared from? How could I tell? The perspective seemed so different by the light of the moon than in daylight. I circled the tombstones, jumping when a clump of tall grass tickled my ankles.

It was as I stepped close to one grass-covered grave, no different in appearance from any of the others that I felt it—the same sensation of withered malignancy that I'd felt in the house. And yet there was something else with it . . . something that I couldn't immediately identify.

"This one, isn't it?" I said, my voice sounding raspy.

"Yes," Russell said staring at me in amazement. "I had to watch from several different vantage points in order to figure it out."

I circled the grave, shining the light from one end to the other. "There's no opening," I said, more to myself than to Russell. "Nowhere for any kind of emanation or emission to come from." Russell might have preferred a ghost to a hallucination, but I'd sooner have discovered a more prosaic explanation.

I focused the beam on the weathered tombstone.

Malachi Bayard. 1785—1854.

The remainder of the inscription was indecipherable.

We retraced our steps to the house and took seats in the living room.

"Drink?" Russell asked, pouring himself a shot of whisky and holding up a second glass.

"No thanks. Gives me a headache," I replied. "Tell me the story. Who was Malachi Bayard?"

Russell downed the whisky in a single gulp and stretched out his legs. "He was a brother of our great-great-great-great-great grandfather. I think I have that right. He lived in this house for some years before building his own place over the hill. It burned down in the early 1900s. He was not, it seems, one of the choicest apples on our somewhat misshapen family tree."

"Rotten to the core?"

"Perhaps not as bad as that," Russell said. "He was the family miser and amassed quite a fortune in various business dealings—some legitimate and others apparently quite shady."

"Rich and unscrupulous?"

"And unpopular. He never married and had few friends. The only one who could tolerate him was his elder brother."

I leaned back in my chair. "You're quite the expert on family history."

"I was fortunate to discover this." Russell leaned to his right, plucked a book off a side table, and handed it to me.

It was leather-bound, with a cracked binding and extensive water staining. I opened it carefully to find yellowing pages covered in immaculate copperplate script.

"It belonged to our five-times removed grandfather," Russell said in answer to my unspoken question. "Cyrus Bayard, older brother to Malachi, and patriarch of the family. It's a diary—a commonplace book, actually. Unfortunately, as you can see, there are pages missing, and many others are damaged. The mice had a field-day with it."

"Wherever did you get it?" I asked.

"I found it stuffed in an old trunk, when I was rummaging in one of the unused rooms,.."

I handed it carefully back to him. "So, what does he have to say about Malachi?"

"Not a lot, actually," Russell smiled ruefully. "Unless there was more on some of the missing pages. But what he did say is interesting."

"Don't keep me in suspense!" I urged.

"Well," Russell said, "Malachi's talents as a noted miser failed to keep the Grim Reaper at bay, and one spring he contracted a chill which developed into pneumonia. I should mention that he had developed the curious habit of wearing a metal box chained to his wrist. He would never divulge the contents. Cyrus believed it contained some kind of charm which Malachi was too afraid or embarrassed to reveal. Anyway, when it dawned on Malachi that he was on his deathbed, he asked

Cyrus to call for a priest."

"A priest?" I echoed.

"Strange, huh? Malachi doesn't seem to have been much of a church-going man, while Cyrus attended the First Reformed Church—now known as the Old Dutch Church. Well, what could Cyrus do but indulge his dying brother? He sent a messenger to fetch the priest. Malachi was well-nigh incoherent at this point, long periods of delirium being interrupted by brief spells of lucidity.

"There are some gaps in the narrative, but it seems that Malachi worsened rapidly, and uttered only a few more words, and those hard to understand." Russell opened the book and turned to one of the yellowed pages. "These were 'poor,' 'bury,' and 'box.' Cyrus took them to mean that Malachi wanted to be buried in a simple grave with his box."

"A reasonable assumption," I said.

Russell nodded. "Well, the priest didn't come. He'd fallen from his horse and broken his leg and was in need of a physician himself. He'd been given enough laudanum that he was in no state of mind to do anything, even if it had been possible to transport him to Malachi's bedside."

He laid the book back on the table. "So there you have it. Malachi died just after 10 p.m. on the third Sunday of June and was buried in the family cemetery. A travelling preacher performed the honors for a nominal fee, since it seemed that no one in town wanted much to do with Malachi. And it wasn't long afterwards that the ghost began appearing, which it has done regularly."

I thought for a moment. "What about Malachi's fortune?"

Russell gave a short laugh. "Who knows? They searched his house from top to bottom and found a fair number of gold coins, but nothing that constituted a fortune."

Something was jiggling in the back of my mind, but I wasn't

sure what.

I yawned, my energy fading. "It's been quite a day. I'd better get some rest."

"Pity you have to leave tomorrow," Russell said.

"Work calls, and I can't afford to retire just yet."

"See you in the morning, then," he said, and I headed upstairs to bed—not that I was expecting to sleep well in this house.

And I didn't.

If the last night had been bad, this one was worse. After lying restless for a while, I must have fallen asleep, because I found myself drifting across a moonlit plain dotted with graves and skeletal, leafless trees, among which other shadowy figures flitted, too transiently for me to obtain more than a glimpse.

I was drawn to one particular grave, but as I approached I saw that it lay open, the earth mounded beside it and nearby a tombstone ready to be erected.

I scanned the eerie landscape, but I was alone. The other shadowy figures had disappeared. I tried to move away, but my dream-body wouldn't respond.

And then a movement arrested my attention. Something was emerging from the dark maw of the grave, something almost, but not quite, human—or had once been human.

It turned a hideous travesty of a face upon me—a face that grew and grew, dwarfing whatever semblance of a body it had possessed, until all I could see was a bottomless pit of a mouth from which mocking laughter erupted.

I swung away, only to confront a second figure rising from another grave and going through the same transformation as the first. I pivoted again and again, but each time another ghastly shape appeared before me, until I was surrounded by a ring of phantom mouths and the dreadful laughter screamed through my brain until I could bear it no more and—

I sat bolt upright in bed, clutching the sheets to my chest, drenched in sweat, peering into the dark corners of the room to assure myself that nothing was there...

And thus I stayed, too frightened to attempt to go back to sleep.

"YOU LOOK AWFUL," Russell said in the morning. "As if you'd seen a ghost."

I returned his feeble effort at humor with a bleary glare. "A bad dream," I said stiffly.

After a quick breakfast he dropped me off at the station.

"Come again, sometime, won't you?" he asked, his blue eyes wistful.

"Sure thing," I replied, mentally vowing that, if I did return to Sleepy Hollow, I'd stay in a motel.

He gave me a quick hug, and I stepped on board the train.

A final wave, and then Sleepy Hollow was disappearing in the distance.

I leaned back in my seat, still puzzling over what continued to jiggle in the back of my mind. It was only as the train approached New York City that I suddenly understood what I had felt at the side of Malachi's grave.

And I thought I should do just as I would have done if a problem arose at work—bring in an expert.

I groped in my pocket for my phone and called Russell's number.

"May I come back next month?" I asked when he answered. "And bring a friend?"

"Certainly," Russell replied. "But who—?"

"Wait and see," I said, yielding to the malicious urge to make him be patient for a change.

IT WAS A MONTH LATER on a Sunday afternoon that, once again, I took the train to Sleepy Hollow. Russell met me at the station. We embraced, then his eyebrows rose as they lit upon my companion—a small, elderly man with a freckled face and thick glasses, the remains of sandy hair turned gray, who walked with a pronounced stoop and, most noticeably, dressed in black clericals and Roman collar.

"Allow me to introduce Father Rider Connor," I said.

Russell shook hands. "I must say, when you said 'a friend' I wasn't expecting an exorcist."

Father Connor chuckled. "Hardly that! I am merely a simple priest who takes an interest in the unusual."

"Father Connor is retired now, but we've known each other for several years," I interjected. "I told him the whole story since I thought he might have some insight into your apparition."

"And do you?" Russell asked the priest.

"I believe so," Father Connor said.

"Well, then," Russell said, "let me take you to the scene."

It wasn't long until we were pulling into the drive to Muh-heakunnetuck Farm.

"A charming location," Father Connor commented appreciatively.

"It suits me," Russell replied. "I'm just not so sure about having a ghost on the premises. Even a family ghost."

"Over there, I presume?" Father Connor gestured towards the cemetery.

Russell nodded.

Father Connor took off at a slow shamble.

Russell gripped my arm and held me back. "Are you sure about this?" he whispered.

"Father Connor is very astute," I whispered back. "And didn't Malachi want a priest to come?"

"A little late now, I should think," Russell retorted.

"Better late than never," I said. A puzzled expression crossed Russell's face.

Father Connor waved us back as we approached the cemetery. "Don't tell me," he said, as he opened the gate and moved among the tombstones.

"This one, I think," he said, finally halting besides Malachi's grave.

"Yes," Russell answered.

Father Connor stood still for a moment, then his eyes met mine. "I believe you're correct," he said.

Russell looked perturbed. "What is it you two can sense that I can't?"

Instead of answering directly, Father Connor said, "We must dig him up."

"Now just a minute!" Russell exclaimed. "We can't do that!"

"Father!" I said, equally shocked.

"We can and we must," Father Connor said.

Russell had gone pale, and I expect I had also.

"Malachi is unquiet," Father Connor added.

"Yes, but he's dead!" I protested. "Can't you just sprinkle a little holy water or something to make him go away?"

"No. There's something holding him back."

"Are you suggesting," Russell waved his hands, searching for words, "that Malachi's spirit is somehow stuck here?"

The priest nodded.

"It's insane!" Russell expostulated. "Jen, tell him!"

I sucked in a breath. Was I going to trust my friend, or not? "Even if Malachi wasn't the most reputable member of our family," I said, addressing myself to Russell, "shouldn't we help him?"

"How do you help a ghost?"

"Fetch a shovel, cousin," I said. "Better yet, two."

At first, I thought he was going to refuse, then he turned

away and headed towards the house, returning in a few minutes with a pair of shovels, one of which he handed to me.

My palms sweaty, I dug mine into the ground, while he hesitated. "Come on, Russell," I said. "Or are you going to let me do all the work?"

With singular lack of enthusiasm, he complied. My heart was racing as I toiled. I felt like a Victorian grave robber. I hoped that Father Connor knew what he was doing.

What would Malachi look like after a century and a half in the ground? Would the climate have preserved him somehow? Or would he be there, all rotten and moldy, decaying like a zombie? I choked back a surge of nausea.

Fortunately, recent rain had made the ground soft, and the digging was fairly easy. Still, my shoulders and arms were aching by the time we reached six feet under, and something that wasn't soil turned up.

Of the coffin, nothing remained but corroded hinges and some discoloration of the earth. And of Malachi himself—to my relief, only disarticulated bones. I averted my gaze from the grinning skull. Looped around one of the forearm bones was a chain, and attached to that, a metal box. My hand trembling, I picked it up and handed it to Father Connor.

"Look," said Russell, "doesn't this amount to desecration?"

Father Connor shook his head. "Quite the opposite."

He knelt by the side of the hole and removed a vial of oil from his pocket.

"The dust returns to the earth as it was," Father Connor said, "and the spirit returns to God who gave it."

He anointed the skull and some of the other bones, reciting the last rites as he did do. When he had finished, he rose, dusted off his knees, and said, "Let's cover him back up."

"Gladly," Russell said, shoveling dirt back into the hole with far more alacrity than he'd removed it.

When it was covered, we traipsed back to the house, where Russell retrieved a hammer and chisel from his toolbox.

"Not just yet." Father Connor laid his hand on the box and slid it away from a surprised Russell. "First, I want you to give me full discretion to deal with the contents of the box as I see fit."

Russell's eyes widened. "That's asking a lot."

"It is," Father Connor said.

Russell looked to me for support.

"Father—" I began.

"I assure you, it's quite necessary," Father Connor said.

After a long moment, Russell shrugged. "What am I going to do with a decrepit old charm, anyway? All right."

"Second," Father Connor said, "let's wait and see what happens tonight."

"In that case," Russell said, apparently having shaken off any adverse effects from the grave-digging, "how about some supper? Pizza OK?"

THE TIME UNTIL ten o'clock seemed to crawl by, despite engaging conversation and an impromptu piano recital by Russell on his Steinway that made me wish that I had practiced more as a youngster and could afford my own.

But, finally, the sun slid behind the hills, and the sky darkened into a cloudless and crystal-clear night.

"Pony up," Russell said at last, and led the way across the meadow, Father Connor and I following. Russell walked stiffly, probably as tense as I was. Father Connor carried a thick black book under one arm, and I noticed his lips moving silently as he limped up the rise.

The graveyard felt even more bleak and desolate at night than it had during the day, the slanting tombstones shining eerily, like a strange, silent congregation somehow waiting for us.

Father Connor walked through the gate. "Coming in?" he asked.

I'd mulled over what I would do. "No," I replied. I don't think anything could have convinced me to pass through that gate.

I clutched the railings and peered into the blackness as the minutes ticked slowly past.

And then it appeared—

IT TURNED TO FACE ME, and for an interminable instant of fear I stared into the distorted visage of what had once been a Bayard, its features warped by endless years of desolation and despair and frustration—

"Russell!" The voice was mine, though seeming to come from far away. "Do you see?"

—before it twisted and turned as it strained upwards, elongating, hands extending into the night sky as if trying to grasp something that was barely out of reach...

And I fancied I heard mocking laughter, as in my dream.

But then, over it, I heard Father Connor's voice, now firm and confident, and the scathing laughter faltered—

The writhing form stretched farther and farther—how long could this go on?—until it reached the point where it could stretch no more, and there it hung, suspended between earth and sky. Surely, as before, it must be sucked back into the ground.

"*Ego absolvo te . . .*"

To my astonishment, the spectral form snapped.

Enveloped in what I can only describe as a golden shimmer, it surged upwards and was gone.

I collapsed against the railings, breathing heavily, conscious of nothing else until a hand touched my trembling shoulder, and I looked around to see Father Connor standing beside me.

"Are you all right?" he asked.

Too shaken to speak, I only nodded.

He held me by one elbow and Russell by the other as we made our way back to the house.

"Now," Father Connor said, sounding business-like, "let's open the box."

It felt like an anticlimax as we sat around the table while Russell, pale and subdued, set to work with his hammer and chisel. A few deft blows shattered the lock, and he pried the lid open.

I gasped as gems poured onto the table. Diamonds, emeralds, rubies . . . a king's ransom.

"The missing fortune!" Russell exclaimed, running his fingers through the gems. "Not a lucky charm after all! Talk about hitting the jackpot!"

"Russell—" I began, imagining myself not having to work anymore, not having to deal with bone-headed administrators whose fantasies outstripped their capital . . .

His glance at me lacked warmth. "Of course, you can have a share as well," he said, in a grudging tone. He neatly divided the pile in two and pushed some towards me.

Father Connor cleared his throat.

We both looked at the priest, who was shaking his head.

Russell's jaw dropped. "But . . ." he stammered, "but you can't. I mean, these are mine . . ."

"They would do you no good," Father Connor said. "You either, Jen."

The look in his eyes was serious. Deadly serious. In my heart I knew he was right.

And yet . . .

"Why not?" Russell asked, his voice harsh.

"What I felt," Father Connor replied, "while standing at the grave, and what Jen also detected, was not only the essence of Malachi's bad deeds but also an impression of remorse."

"I don't see Malachi as the repenting type," Russell scoffed.

"Nevertheless, he performed the uncharacteristic action of sending for a priest on his deathbed," Father Connor pointed out, "which implies some change of heart. And remember Malachi's last recorded words," he added, his focus shifting between us. "'Poor,' 'box,' and 'bury.' Everyone assumed that they meant he desired to be buried with his box. But taken together, these things suggested to me that he wanted to be rid of the box—that he didn't intend it to be buried with him at all. Unfortunately, in his state, he was unable to communicate his desires in an understandable manner. And so, he was buried as we found him."

"It's crazy," Russell said.

"Not at all," Father Connor countered. "I am convinced that Malachi realized what his attachment to wealth had done to him and desired the contents of his box to be given to the poor. And that is exactly what I shall do with them."

His gaze took in both of us. "There will not be another Malachi." He reached out to sweep the gems away.

"No," Russell said. His cheeks flushed as he blocked the priest's move. "This is a plot, isn't it? Jen, how could you? You knew what was in the box, and you're trying to rob me!"

For a moment, I wavered. What I could do with the money those gems would provide . . .

And I felt Muhheakunnetuck Farm gloating, as if those ancient walls were shaking with derisive laughter, and all those warped and twisted scions of the family tree were reaching out to embrace me into their perverse fold . . .

In my mind's eye, I was back in the cemetery, observing the struggles of a blighted spirit, confronted by that haunted face with its tormented eyes and expression of sheer hopelessness . . . and I shuddered, realizing the awful fate that lurked for me in the darkness of my own soul.

And not only me.

"He's right, Russell," I said, forcing myself to speak. "Did you see, tonight, the face . . . ?"

"No," he said, in a tone that made me doubt his veracity.

I reached out and with quivering fingers slid my portion of the gems over to Father Connor.

"I did," I said, uncomfortably aware that I possessed more than the Bayard physiognomy, "and in it I saw my own!"

SIX
The Lady of the Island

"I DON'T BELIEVE IN PHANTOM ISLANDS," SAID THE professor-type sunk into a worn armchair near the blazing fire in the Three Horseshoes. Bledsoe wasn't actually a professor— he managed a local bank—but, as a man who fancied his own erudition, felt it incumbent upon himself to impart the benefits of his learning to all and sundry, their desire for knowledge or lack thereof notwithstanding.

"Not another lecture, Bledsoe," somebody groaned. "Can't we talk about football?"

A chorus of agreement met this suggestion.

Outside, pouring rain lashed the solid stone-work of the inn while gusts of wind worked the oak trees into a frenzy of flailing branches, ripping off leaves and flinging them into the darkness of the night. Driving home along narrow, winding roads in the pitch black in such weather held little appeal, and so the patrons stayed put, sipping perry or bitters and hoping the storm would abate before the landlord called time and evicted every last man into Mother Nature's inclement hands.

"I mean," Bledsoe continued, ignoring the objection and raking his eyes over the dozen or so occupants of the lounge, "that there's a natural explanation for them. Navigational error, for example, or volcanic activity, or erosion, or hoaxes."

Why he suddenly brought this up was a mystery, because until then the conversation had been desultory, consisting mostly of local gossip. Nobody, it seemed, had the energy or desire to engage in prolonged discussion—thus presenting

Bledsoe with a prime opportunity to offer enlightenment.

He opened his mouth to continue, when he was forestalled.

"I disagree," said an old man tucked into a corner. He was wiry, wearing a faded tan-colored cable-knit sweater pulled up to the stubble of his chin. White hair peeked from under a flat cap, and the hands holding a mug of steaming tea were gnarled. His eyes, though, were bright, with a sort of curious gleam, both penetrating and benevolent. He wasn't a regular like the rest of us, but, while it wasn't common, neither was it unheard of for a passerby to happen upon the Three Horseshoes and avail himself of country hospitality. How long he had been sitting unnoticed in the corner was another mystery.

"And I suppose you know something about it?" Bledsoe scoffed, obviously irritated.

The other drank from his mug. "Considering that I single-handedly circumnavigated the world, I might be judged to have some knowledge of the matter."

"You have a story?" a young workman asked, once a flurry of half-stifled laughter had subsided, followed by a shuffling of feet and chairs as everyone maneuvered closer to listen, to Bledsoe's further annoyance.

"Aye," the visitor said, staring challengingly at Bledsoe, "but I doubt if you'll believe me."

"Probably not," Bledsoe said.

"Don't be put off by him," the workman—Carter—said, as another blast of wind shuddered the windows and howled around the chimney. "Tell us your story."

"Please do," seconded Father Dennis of St. Dunstan's, who had stopped by for a pint and stayed to dry his feet at the fire.

Finding himself outnumbered, Bledsoe raised his hands in reluctant surrender.

The old man—who hadn't introduced himself—set down his mug on a window ledge.

"It was many years ago, when I was young and hale," he commenced. "I'd always loved the sea, and I'd recently read Captain Joshua Slocum's book. Do you know it?"

"Of course," said Bledsoe quickly. "*Sailing Alone Around the World.*"

"That's the one," the old man affirmed. "If Slocum could do it, why couldn't I?"

"Perhaps because he was a professional sailor," Bledsoe suggested snidely.

A smile flickered across the visitor's lips. "To be sure, he had that advantage. I won't burden you with the details, but I found myself a nice little sloop named the *Seastar*, learned how to sail her, bought a boat-load of maps and charts, loaded her with provisions, and set off on the adventure of a lifetime."

He chuckled. "I was young and foolish. Had I been older and wiser, I wouldn't be telling you this story."

The landlord brought out more bottles of perry and bitters and propped himself against the wall within earshot.

"Crossing the Atlantic was a painful learning experience, but I made it. Then I took my time cruising down the American coast and across the Caribbean. I could have gone through the Panama Canal, but since Slocum had rounded Cape Horn, I was foolish enough to follow in his wake. How I survived, I'll never know. The Good Lord must have been watching over me Himself—either that, or some poor angel was decidedly busy. But that's another story. Suffice it to say that it was three months and some near wrecks before I cleared the Straits of Magellan and found myself idling through the south Pacific, with dreams of palm-shaded islands and beautiful girls floating through my mind."

"Sounds delightful," said Carter.

"What I didn't know," the old man said, waving away Carter's comment, "was that a typhoon was heading my way.

Fortunately, I only caught the edge of it, otherwise I'd have vanished without a trace, like so many ships and men before me—or like one of the islands my skeptical friend here doesn't believe in.

"The *Seastar* was a tough little ship, but she took an awful pounding. Those days and nights were some of the longest of my life. You think it's a storm outside tonight—well, you don't know what a real storm is until you've ridden out a typhoon in the middle of the Pacific, with waves taller than houses tossing you about like you were a piece of foam, and the wind whipping the spray until you could hardly tell which was water and which was air.

"To go on deck would have been suicide. I stayed below, struggling to wedge myself in my bunk so as not to be dashed to pieces, and praying for my life every moment. Sleep was out of the question. Many a time I thought the *Seastar* was going under, never to surface again."

He reached under his shirt and pulled out a worn gold crucifix.

"This is the same one I was wearing then. Some people think it's a sign of weakness to pray, but I'm not ashamed to say that Samuel Hoskins was scared."

His gaze ran over the assembled men as if daring them to contradict him, but nobody spoke.

"Not, mind you," he added, "that I've always been very good about praying. In fact, there were a great many things I wasn't good at—and many things I was good at that I shouldn't have been."

The door rattled, and a gust of wind swept through the room as it opened to admit the entrance of a sodden man wearing a heavy raincoat. The landlord left to attend to the new arrival.

"When the storm finally blew over, the *Seastar* was rolling in the swell with her sails and rigging in tatters, and her mast snapped off. Worse, she'd sprung a leak—I plugged it as well as

I could, but still had a job to bail her out. When I figured she was dry enough to stay afloat for a while, I went back on deck to try to determine my position—not always an easy task in those days before satellites and GPS.

"When I'd figured it out and consulted my charts, it turned out that I was quite literally in the middle of nowhere—no land for hundreds of miles in any direction."

"No islands of beautiful girls?" asked Bledsoe sarcastically.

"No islands of any sort," the old man replied. "I'd have taken an island of ugly men if they could have helped. For I was in dire straits. My water stores had been contaminated, and my food wasn't much better. And with the passing of the typhoon, the sun was blazing hot and the breeze had dropped to a mere whisper. I was going to be very uncomfortable. I scanned the sea looking for another ship, but it was empty to the horizon. My radio was wrecked, so I couldn't call for help.

"There was nothing to do but rig up some scraps of sail to the stump of the mast, and hope that the currents or the breeze would carry me towards a shipping lane. And so I drifted for several days, bailing out the *Seastar*, trying to catch a few fish, and getting thirstier by the day."

He retrieved his mug and held it up; the landlord, having returned, took the hint and refilled it. The young workman laid another log on the fire.

"The island?" prompted Bledsoe.

"Patience, man, I'm coming to it," Hoskins rejoined with a touch of asperity. "By then I was fairly exhausted and fell into a deep sleep—if the *Seastar* had taken on water and sunk, I should not have been able to do anything about it.

"When morning came, I crawled on deck with my binoculars, hoping to spot a passing ship. Instead, to my surprise, I saw land—the dim outline of an island upon the horizon. At first, I thought I must be hallucinating, or seeing a cloud bank—"

"Exactly," the doubter said, earning a glare from the old man.

"—but viewing the island gave me renewed vigor and I re-checked my position most carefully. There was not supposed to be land anywhere near me. Thankfully, the breeze had picked up and was carrying the *Seastar* towards the island. Some while later when I could examine it more closely, I estimated it to be five or six miles long, and perhaps as far away. Hilly, but not mountainous.

"I tell you, I had never seen anything as beautiful as that dark green island arising from the blue of the sea, highlighted by the white of breakers. If only the wind would hold ...

"And it did. Hour by hour the *Seastar* drew closer, as if directed by a divine hand towards a break in the reef. Just a gentle touch upon the rudder kept her as straight as an arrow. And the fragrance ... I had never before smelled anything so wonderful as the breath of the mountains and the trees.

"The clouds were bright with the reds and golds of sunset as the *Seastar* glided through the break in the reef and into a calm lagoon, where she grounded gently upon a beach of dazzling white sand. There was probably no need to drop the anchor, but I did, then leaped overboard and splashed onto the beach, where I fell to my knees, running the sand through my fingers, and thanking God for my good fortune.

"I had seen no signs of life as I approached, but, just to be safe, I slept on board the *Seastar* with my rifle close at hand. When morning came, I was in no hurry to make repairs—my first thought was to find a source of water and, if possible, food.

"Water I located fairly soon, as a stream trickled down from a nearby hill, emptying not far from the beach. I drank my fill, then rinsed and refilled all my water containers. Palm trees supplied coconuts for my breakfast.

"Feeling somewhat refreshed, and despite my wobbly sea-legs, I put my rifle over my shoulder and set off to explore. I should say that I have never been a good shot, either then or now, and frankly detested the thought of shooting some innocent beast, but since my own survival was at stake I might have to attempt it. Besides, there might have been wild dogs or some other dangerous creatures.

"But I saw and heard nothing but a few brightly-colored birds flying in the canopy of the trees. The silence was profound—only the rustle of leaves and the distant roar of the surf. I could have been the only man on the island—perhaps even the first, for I saw nothing to indicate that anyone had ever set foot here before. 'Hoskins' Island' I thought to name it when I returned to civilization."

"How modest of you," murmured the skeptic.

"We'd all have done the same," countered the young workman. "Except perhaps for Father Dennis here," he added, indicating the parish priest.

After the laughter had died down, Hoskins resumed.

"And yet I had a strange feeling that for all my isolation I wasn't alone. There was nothing upon which to base such a feeling, but there it was."

"A psychiatric disturbance, no doubt," said Bledsoe, yawning.

Hoskins was undeterred. "I decided to climb the hill to take better stock of the island. The climb was easy, but because of my weakened condition I was nearly exhausted by the time I reached the summit. Once there, though, I was rewarded with one of the most beautiful views I have ever seen. Not far off was an inland lake of the clearest azure, shining like a crystal. It was fringed with palm trees, and in its center was a fair-sized, tree-dotted island, linked to the shore by an isthmus of land. I thought I glimpsed a structure of some sort in the midst of the trees, but I couldn't be sure. I reached for my binoculars before remembering that I'd left them on the *Seastar*.

"My curiosity was well-aroused, and I determined to investigate it at close range, and so I descended the hill, making my way towards the lake.

"As I drew closer, I heard a crackling in the underbrush and dropped to one knee, my rifle at my shoulder, my finger tensed upon the trigger. I was shocked when an English voice said, 'You won't need that dreadful thing. Put it away,' and a woman stepped out into the open."

"I knew it!" Carter laughed. "Was she naked?"

"No," Hoskins said, "she was wearing a long, flowing robe of what looked like white silk with silver threads. She was tall and slender and had an absolutely perfect face, framed by long, flaxen hair. Her eyes were of the softest grey. I felt as though I were seeing a vision. I was utterly astounded—"

"And fell down in worship," Carter suggested.

"Not quite," Hoskins corrected. "For the first and only time in my life, I fainted."

"What an anticlimax!" Carter chortled.

"It didn't feel so at the time … for I found myself back on the *Seastar*, being flung around and battered into near-oblivion. The noise was incredible—as if all the fury of the storm had been translated into sound, tearing through my very body. It seemed to last for an eternity. And just when I felt I could endure it no longer, the *Seastar* plunged—down and down she went, into a black abyss bereft of sound, the silence even more terrifying than the noise had been. I could see her stout timbers bulging under the immense pressure, bowing inwards, farther and farther. The wood creaked and groaned, and then split with a crack like a thunderclap. The cold, black ocean rushed in, and I screamed with my last breath as it overwhelmed me and everything went dark.

"When I became aware again, I felt as though I was floating upon a cloud, while from the distance came the strains of ethereal music. Well, I was dead, and that was all there was to it."

"Glad to hear it," grumbled Bledsoe.

A shriek of wind and rain hitting the windowpanes like hail obliterated Hoskins' response.

When it subsided, he said, "I opened my eyes, to find that I was lying on a cushioned divan, shielded from the sun by a canopy. A cool cloth was over my forehead, and a light sheet covered my body. Beside me on a table was a pitcher of water, a glass, and a plate of fruit. I realized I was hungry and thirsty and availed myself of both. Then I stood up. 'Hello!' I called. 'Is anybody here?' Instantly, the music—it had been a woman singing—stopped. And a moment later, the woman I had seen walked under the canopy.

"'You're real!' I gasped, once again mesmerized by her beauty.

"'Of course I am,' she smiled, and it struck me how foolish I must have sounded.

"'Where am I?' I asked, the questions tumbling out. 'What place is this? How did I get here? Who are you?'

"'To take the last, first,' she replied, 'my name is Lilian. This is my island, and,' she added, indicating the divan and the canopy with a wave of a shapely arm, 'I brought you here.'

"She hardly looked strong enough to carry me, but I didn't wish to argue with her.

"My head swam and I sat back down. 'Don't move too quickly,' she said. 'You've been lying in bed with a fever for the past week.'

"I could well believe it. 'You've been caring for me?' I asked.

"'Yes,' she said, 'day and night.'

"'Are you alone here?' I queried.

"'I have one friend,' she answered, and for the first time I noticed an impressive, coal-black, wolf-like dog that stood behind her, with erect ears and brown eyes that regarded me with intelligence but not, I hoped, hostility. I must have gulped, because she said, 'Don't worry. Shadow won't hurt you."

"'I had a dog named Shadow when I was young,' I said.

"'I did, too,' she replied sadly, 'But I didn't treat him well.'

"That seemed odd coming from the mouth of so lovely a creature.

"Then she gave a small smile. 'You are wondering why a woman is alone on an island, and whether she misses human company.'

"I nodded, for those were exactly my thoughts.

"She regarded me with her head tipped to one side. 'That is part of—' She broke off abruptly. 'But let us not talk of that.' She turned aside to forestall my obvious next question, laid her hand on the big dog's head, and said, 'Follow me.'

"I rose, feeling more stable this time. A few steps along a stone path brought us to a small cottage set in a garden beside jeweled waters. I realized that we were now on the island in the center of the inland lake. The cottage was fashioned of blocks of coral surmounted by a thatched roof topped by a chimney. A pair of neat gables protruded from under the overhang of the thatch, and a bay window looked out over the garden. A porch ran around two sides, ivy climbed the walls, and blooming flowers were arranged in neat beds on either side of a wooden door. The whole effect was charming in the extreme. It appeared so European that I wondered who had built it and when.

"The path skirted the cottage, and Lilian directed me to a small outbuilding. 'You may stay here while you work on your boat,' she said. "You will find all the materials and tools you require.'

"'How do you know about my boat?' I asked, but she favored me with a mysterious expression and made no answer. I looked through the door to see a well-stocked workshop, and in one corner a neatly made bed.

"'I don't know how to thank you,' I said.

"'There is no need,' she replied. 'You will join Shadow and me for supper?'

"'I would be delighted,' I said, 'although my clothes are rather the worse for wear.'

"She laughed. 'Come as you are. There will be no one to write up the account in the society papers.'

Accompanied by Shadow, she departed, and I sat upon the bed to marvel at my good fortune. I had wondered how to repair the *Seastar* well enough to cover thousands more miles of open ocean, and here my prayers had been answered in a most amazing manner."

"I don't believe a word of it," Bledsoe said, sitting upright.

"It's true," Hoskins rejoined, taking a swallow of his tea. "Everything."

"I suppose you had a camera and took photographs," Bledsoe persisted.

"I had a camera," Hoskins replied, "but it perished in the typhoon, much to my regret."

"So we have only your word."

"Let him finish," Father Dennis said.

"Aye, shut the trap, Bledsoe," seconded Carter. The banker glowered and subsided back into his chair.

"Lilian proved to be a charming dinner companion," Hoskins resumed, "able to converse on any number of subjects, but one—herself. She deflected all my inquiries. By the time dinner had ended, I knew no more about her then when it had begun. She, though, knew rather more about me.

"I told her how I'd grown up in a wealthy family, and never had to worry about finding employment. How I lived for excitement—I lived just to live! I told her about my travels aboard the *Seastar*, the places I had visited.

"She regarded me gravely, seeing, I believe, better than I saw myself, the restlessness that drove me. But I didn't realize that at the time—it only dawned upon me later.

"I slept exceedingly well that night and the next day felt fully restored. After breakfast—which I found beside my bed when I awoke—I decided to make a start upon repairing the *Seastar*. Trailed by Shadow—for the big dog seemed determined to keep a watchful eye on me—I returned to my sloop and gave her a thorough going over, from bowsprit to stern. I made detailed notes and measurements of everything I would need. Plugging the leak and repairing the mast were my priorities, followed by making new sails and repairing the rigging. The cabin needed to be made shipshape again and dried out. Once those tasks were completed, I could replenish my stores and be ready to resume my adventure.

"Fortunately, I had spare spar, extra canvas and rope, and anything else I needed I discovered in Lilian's workshop. And so, the next couple of weeks developed a routine—I would work on the *Seastar* for as long as I was able, rest when I needed to, and dine with Lilian, who faithfully provided all my meals. After the first few days, Shadow ceased to pay me much heed and was continually with Lilian—accompanying her when sometimes she would come to see me at work, lying by her feet at meals, and—as she told me—sleeping beside her bed at night.

"I need not say that as the days passed my feelings for my charming hostess intensified. I daresay no man alive could have resisted falling in love with her. But something held me back from expressing my sentiments. After all, what had I to offer her—she who had a perfect if solitary life here? She would not, I thought be tempted by a life of luxury in England. She was not the type to court Society—in fact, she seemed distressed when I would talk about my family connections."

"You have connections?" Bledsoe said, stroking his

mustache.

"We are talking of a time many years ago," Hoskins replied.

"Don't judge a book by its cover, mate," one of the other men interjected.

"But nothing could keep me from dreaming," Hoskins said. "Oh, the dreams I had of her . . ." His voice trailed off for a moment. "It was during this time that something very unusual occurred," he said. "After wrestling for some hours with a very recalcitrant piece of iron—I was refashioning a broken cleat—I decided to go for a walk. Lilian's cottage, as I said, was surrounded by gardens interspersed with copses of trees. There was one part of the gardens to which I had not ventured, and to this I made my way. I am not a gardener and have no knowledge of plants, and so I have no idea of the identity of the multicolored blooms through which I wandered.

"But suddenly they parted and I was facing a gleaming white obelisk. It appeared to be made of marble and had three sides. In the center of the side before which I stood was a carving. I confess, gentlemen, that it gave me pause. Never in my life had I seen anything so ugly, so repulsive, so disturbing as that face that stared back at me. I assumed, because of its long hair, that it was a woman—but what a hag! The mouth was twisted and distorted, the nose misshapen, the teeth rotten, and the eyes— oh, the eyes! They gleamed with a maliciousness that was at once cold, mocking, cunning, and acquisitive. I shuddered, wondering what such a monstrosity was doing here in paradise.

"Half afraid, I ventured to the next side. And there—I saw Lilian! But it was not Lilian as I knew her—it was Lilian as if portrayed by a grossly inferior sculptor. It was recognizable, yes, but oddly, as if the proportions weren't quite right. Yet her eyes were gentle and she was smiling—if, I thought, somewhat wistfully.

"And on the third side, was Lilian in perfection—exquisitely proportioned, her eyes alight, her smile joyful. So real ... so vibrant ..."

"How interesting," mused Father Dennis, one hand on his chin.

"Confounded ridiculous," said Bledsoe.

Hoskins cleared his throat. "I was perplexed as to what to make of this curious obelisk. But more than that, I suddenly felt uneasy, as if I trespassed on some sort of sacred ground where I had no right to be. And so, I hurried away, looking around to make sure that Lilian hadn't observed me.

"I thought she regarded me curiously at dinner that night— as if she knew, or suspected—and once or twice I almost asked about the obelisk, but I didn't.

"And so, life went on as usual for the next few days, until at last the *Seastar* was as sea-worthy as I could make her. I'd rigged up a pulley and by dint of great effort winched her off the beach where I'd grounded her. What a pretty sight she was, floating in the placid lagoon! I was eager to set sail—to return to the life I knew—and yet I quailed at the thought of leaving Lilian.

"'The *Seastar* is ready. Come with me,' I begged her at dinner that final night, but she shook her head.

"'That can never be.'

"'Am I so awful?' I asked.

"'You have far to journey,' she replied, 'and it is not given to me to accompany you.' I tried to persuade her, but she was immune to all my arguments. And so, it was with a heavy heart that I went to bed that night and with a heavy heart that I arose in the morning. It was a beautiful day, cloudless, with a breeze perfect to speed the *Seastar* on her way.

"Lilian, accompanied by Shadow, met me as I was packing up a few belongings. Once again, I implored her to come with me, and once again she refused. I realized that my arguments would be fruitless. It was then that I asked her—'Does it have something to do with the obelisk?'

"'So you've seen it?' she replied. 'I thought perhaps so.'

"'I was wandering around one day when I stumbled upon it. If it was wrong of me, I apologize . . .'"

"'No,' she replied, 'I rather thought you might. Let me explain.'

"She beckoned me to follow, and we made our way through the gardens to the obelisk, Shadow padding behind.

"'It seems a very strange object to be here,' I said, when we arrived at the clearing.

"'Not really,' she replied. 'It's my tomb.'

"Her words took me aback, and I'm afraid that I stood there with my mouth open. 'You hope to be buried here?' I said at last.

"'No,' she replied. 'I am buried here.'

"'That's insane!' I gasped. 'You're—you're very much alive.'

"'Not as you think.'

"'I don't understand,' I said.

Bledsoe coughed. "I don't know that I want to."

"I do," countered Father Dennis. "Please go on, Hoskins."

The old man nodded. "'Let me tell you about myself,' she said. 'I was raised by very devout parents; so devout, in fact, that they desired for me to enter a convent. My older brother had become a priest, and they hoped that I would be as devoted to the faith as he. But I was a very headstrong young woman, determined to go my own way. I rapidly departed from the faith my parents had instilled in me—I saw it as an impediment to the life I wished to live. And so, I became a very modern woman, in the worst sense of the word. The details don't matter, but, had you met me then, you would have found a very selfish, self-centered person. I was cruel, unforgiving, and prideful. And eventually my pride cost an innocent young man his life.

"'And then my own mortality confronted me. In the prime of life, I contracted scarlet fever. At that time, the doctors could do nothing. It was on my deathbed that I repented of the life I had lived and the harm that I had caused. My sins, you see, were very great.'

"'Surely not!' I exclaimed, thinking that so beautiful a creature could not be guilty of such wickedness.

"'You see this portrait,' she said, indicating the ghastly crone on the first side of the obelisk. 'This was the state of my soul when I died.'

"I stared aghast at the hideous, deformed image.

"'A travesty of what I should have been,' she said, moving around to place her hand on the third, the perfect side.

"I remained rooted in place, my mind whirling. 'And the middle portrait?' I asked.

"'It represents where I am now,' Lilian said.

"And as I studied that middle portrait again, I saw that it had changed from when I had viewed it previously. The proportions were better, the smile more radiant... I blinked, to make sure my eyes weren't deceiving me.

"'It's different!' I exclaimed.

"'So you see,' Lilian said, 'you have helped me, even as I have aided you. Thanks to your fortuitous arrival on my island, my journey of reparation has taken another step.'

"'Was it fortuitous?' I wondered, suddenly having a small inkling into the matter.

"But she only smiled, laid a hand on my arm and, with Shadow beside her, conducted me to the *Seastar*.

"My heart was torn as I climbed aboard, while she remained standing on the beach.

"'Godspeed, Samuel,' she said, waving as I raised anchor, hoisted sail, and steered the *Seastar* towards the opening in the breakers and the wide ocean that lay beyond.

"'Goodbye, Lilian,' I called in response. 'I will return to you.'

"I had to concentrate on guiding the *Seastar* safely past the breakers. When she was clear, I looked back, but the beach was deserted. The breeze carried me swiftly away, and when some little while later, I turned around for one last view of the island, it was to see that it too had vanished."

Carter let out his breath. "Did you go back?" he asked.

"I tried," Hoskins said, picking up his mug. "I had taken the coordinates carefully and written them down in my logbook. But when I returned perhaps a year later, there was nothing but empty ocean." His blue eyes fixed on the banker.

"Rubbish!" exclaimed Bledsoe angrily. "Pure unmitigated rubbish!"

"Not at all," said Father Dennis quietly.

"Do you mean to say that you believe this fantasy?" Bledsoe said, springing upright.

"Yes," replied the priest.

"Well, I don't," Bledsoe said, bringing his fist down on the armrest of his chair. "It's nonsense. Making amends for wrong deeds? Humbug! The universe doesn't care about our notions of right and wrong. It's indifferent. And as for God, angels, spirits, and whatever—I don't believe in them."

"You should," said the old man, with sudden passion in his voice.

"You really should," he repeated, his face curiously appearing to be that of a much younger man. And with those words he abruptly vanished and his mug clattered to the stone floor.

SEVEN
The House Without a Song

"I HOPE YOU'LL LIKE ARDY CHARLTON," I SAID TO Devin as we mounted the weathered, moss-covered steps of WestRiver House, situated in a fold of the hills not far from Chipping Campden. "But I wish you'd met him years ago. He's never been the same since Margo died."

I groped through a profusion of ivy in order to locate and ring the doorbell. From deep inside came the faint notes of the Westminster Chimes.

"Why didn't he remarry?" Devin asked.

"He said that no one could live up to Margo," I answered.

Devin sighed and waved a hand to indicate the house. "Can you believe this?"

"It used to be neat," I replied. But the ivy had been left to run riot until it covered the warm Cotswold stone and dangled over the mullioned windows, leaving only narrow strips of glass visible. The top of a chimney peeked over the green mass.

The door rattled and opened. A slender, black-clad figure with thinning hair and rimless glasses appeared in the opening.

"Caeden!" he exclaimed. "Welcome. And this must be Devin. Come in, come in."

He moved aside to allow us entrance.

"Good to see you again, Ardy," I said, shaking the offered hand. "You haven't aged a bit."

"Liar," he laughed, although it wasn't the hearty laugh of old, but a joyless, tired imitation. He took my coat and hung it on a rack, then performed the same service with Devin's jacket.

"It's a pity Helen couldn't make it," he said.

"She's visiting family in Aberdeen," I answered, not deeming it necessary to inform him that my wife had departed in a fit of anger. Her job had been unusually stressful lately, I'd been fretting about sluggish book sales, and what should have been a reasoned discussion had gone very badly awry.

"We can't afford a new car!" I'd protested.

"But my old one isn't safe anymore!" Helen had retorted. "It's a death trap! Why don't you drive it?"

"Don't exaggerate! You're always making mountains out of molehills..."

The slamming of the door had punctuated her final words: "Money and yourself! That's all you think about!"

Ardy escorted me and Devin down a paneled hallway towards the living room. As we passed, I couldn't help but glance at the base of the staircase that curved upwards to the landing. The staircase where—

I tore my eyes away and instead regarded the fire crackling in the Adam fireplace. Despite the glowing ambiance, the house felt as cheerless as the last time I'd been here. It was as if the life had drained out of it, leaving only the shell of what had once been a home. I couldn't tell if Devin sensed it, but to me, who had pleasant memories of visiting here in happier times, it was almost painful. If even Buster, the dog, were still here...

The interior, though, appeared unchanged. Bookcases lined the walls, alternating with curio cabinets crammed with a veritable museum-load of Mesopotamian artifacts. Persian rugs cushioned our footfalls, and a dusty crystal chandelier hung overhead. Flanked by a pair of Assyrian statues—fierce-faced men with long, curly beards—a Steinway grand piano dominated the center of the room.

On it stood a photograph of a woman, her attractive face framed by waves of chestnut-colored hair, her green eyes shining, and a smile curving her lips.

I showed it to Devin, mouthing the name "Margo." Devin nodded, and I set it down again.

As I did so, a figure seated in the dimness of a drape-shaded bay window rose from an armchair.

"You remember my cousin, Holly, don't you?" Ardy said.

"I most certainly do." I took the woman's hand. She was fiftyish, tall, and elegant, wearing a cashmere sweater and an abundance of jangling bracelets. "I enjoyed your last volume of poetry immensely."

"Thank you, Caeden," she said, brushing back a bang from her high forehead. "I can't wait to get my hands on your latest novel. A New York Times bestseller?"

"Probably not even a local bestseller," I grumbled. "But I have advance copies in my bag and will be delighted to offer you one." I turned to usher Devin forwards. "My friend Devin Everist. A man of no literary accomplishments, but an excellent tennis player."

"Not to mention being an astute literary agent," Devin said, giving me a mock glare before turning a smile on Holly. "Pleased to meet you, Miss Giffin."

"You know of Holly?" I asked.

"Of course," Devin said nonchalantly. "I don't represent poetry—or read it, either, I must confess—but I'm aware of the name."

"Good enough," Holly said.

Devin turned to Ardy. "The idea crossed my mind that perhaps you'd pen a novel, based on your researches."

Ardy let out a gusty sigh and averted his gaze. "Look to Caeden," he said. "I have no inclination."

"But surely with your knowledge and Caeden's command of fiction—" Devin began, ignoring a warning shake of the head from me.

"The subject is not open for discussion," Ardy said harshly. "And if you insist, I shall have to ask you to leave."

Devin's jaw dropped. "I'm sorry," he mumbled after an awkward moment. "I meant no offense."

Ardy held up a hand. "Perhaps Caeden didn't make my situation clear to you. I have written nothing—nothing—since the loss of my wife. And I am tired of well-wishing friends and acquaintances trying to encourage me to do something that I have absolutely no desire to do. The pen has been stilled. Forever."

He turned his hand palm up in a conciliatory gesture. "As long as that is clear . . ."

"It is," Devin said.

"Good. Then let us talk of other things." Ardy motioned us to chairs. "May I offer you a glass of wine before dinner?"

"Certainly," Holly answered, seconded by Devin and myself. Ardy disappeared into the kitchen.

"I didn't mean to offend him," Devin whispered to me. "I didn't think he'd be so touchy."

"For heaven's sake, just don't mention it again," I whispered back. "Anything to do with Margo is a sensitive subject."

Ardy reappeared with a tray containing four wine glasses. "This is a Welsh Madeleine Angevine of which I'm rather fond. I hope you enjoy it."

After handing out glasses, he set the tray down on a table and subsided into a deep chair. It almost swallowed him, and I wondered how much more weight he had lost.

"Is your latest novel like your previous one, Caeden? Based on autobiographical material?"

"There's some," I replied, sipping the wine. "This is quite good, Ardy. But most of the book is the product of my imagination."

"He has an *outré* side," Devin said.

"I should call Caeden's genius quirky or unusual," Holly

85

said, "not bizarre or outlandish. Have you discovered any new imaginative authors, Devin?"

"Not as many as I would like," he replied. "It's all vampires and zombies and other derivative stuff."

"A sign of the times," Ardy sighed. "I don't know how you manage to wade through it, Devin. You must encounter some awful dreck."

"The bottom line," Devin answered. "If I think it might sell, I'll read it."

We chatted for a while longer, until Ardy's housekeeper appeared to announce that dinner was ready, and we traipsed into the dining room. I hadn't been quite sure what to expect; Margo had been the one to organize dinner parties in the old days, always careful to achieve the correct proportion of guests—balancing her more artistic friends with Ardy's academic ones. I fell somewhere in the middle, being an author on one hand, but an old school friend of Ardy's on the other. I think that her motto had been "When in doubt, invite Caeden."

But visits to WestRiver house had become rare since Ardy's innate reclusive tendencies had been allowed to flourish unopposed. I'd gathered from other mutual acquaintances that he barely left the house, other than to attend Sunday Mass. He'd disappeared from the academic scene.

And so, I'd been mildly surprised when his message had arrived, inviting Helen and me.

Helen. I glanced to my right.

It wasn't the same having Devin seated beside me.

How was Helen faring up there in Aberdeen?

Ardy's housekeeper proved to be a more-than-able cook, serving us a nicely seasoned London broil with carrots and mashed potatoes, followed by an apple pie and custard. Ardy made a commendable effort to be the good host, although he ate little and his conversation struck me as being somewhat forced.

I noticed that he had developed the habit of cocking his head to one side, in the direction of the living room, as if listening for something.

After dinner, Ardy and I were deep in discussion over snifters of brandy, while Holly and Devin had preceded us back to the coziness of the fire. All of a sudden, over the clink of the housekeeper washing the dishes in the kitchen, came a few notes from the grand piano.

The effect on Ardy was electric. He broke off in midsentence and dashed from the room. I hastened to catch up.

Devin was seated at the piano. "Rubinstein's *Melodie in F*," he said, glancing up from the music on the rack. "A charming salon piece. Do you play, Ardy?"

I interposed myself between the two men as Holly intervened and caught hold of Devin's hands.

"Ardy doesn't play," I said. "The piano was Margo's."

Devin flushed and rose hastily from the bench. "I'm dreadfully sorry. I keep making a muddle of things. Perhaps... perhaps I should go..."

"It's my fault, Ardy," I interjected. "I forgot to mention the piano... it escaped my mind that Devin played."

Ardy took a deep breath. At first, I thought he was going to lose his temper, but when he spoke it was calmly, and to Devin.

"That won't be necessary," he said, smoothing the pages of the Rubinstein and straightening it next to a closed copy of Vaughan Williams' Songs of Travel. "But the piano is not to be played... nobody must ever play it except Margo."

Devin looked puzzled.

"I didn't tell him everything," I said to Ardy. "Out of respect for your privacy."

"Then I must," Ardy said.

He perched on the edge of the bench; Devin headed for the couch, Holly retreated to her chair by the fireplace, while I leaned against the Steinway.

"I was not the best of husbands," Ardy said without preamble. "I was the stereotypical academic, absorbed in my work, tolerating interruptions and disturbance poorly, and at times totally blind to the quite different needs of my wife. She, as Caeden can attest, was my opposite. Whereas I was quiet and reserved, she was outgoing. She liked to talk, I to read. She could multi-task with ease, I not at all."

He fingered the sheet music on the rack. "She loved to play the piano and sing. The *Melodie in F* was one of her favorites. She was an excellent pianist with a fine voice. And her repertoire was varied, from Schubert to Vaughan Williams." He touched the *Songs of Travel.* "It was her habit after dinner to play and sing."

"I remember well," Holly said quietly, and I nodded in quiet recollection of those vanished days.

"But I was not appreciative," Ardy said, "especially when I was working. If I was deep in concentration then I found her singing to be distracting. My study is through there,"—he pointed out a doorway to Devin—"and although this house is old and well-built, I could easily hear her."

He took his glasses off, studied them for a moment, then put them back on.

"Ardy," I said, "you don't have to—"

He motioned me to silence. "One night," he said, "I was working on a cuneiform text relating to the reign of Ashurbanipal, the last strong king of Assyria, and having a devilishly tough time of it. I shouldn't have been doing it—I was tired after a long day, had a headache, and ought to have made myself a toddy and gone to bed. But I was being stubborn.

"Margo was singing something she'd heard on the radio, trying to recall it from memory. I don't even know what it was, just that it had several high notes. The first time, I didn't mind. But after the third or fourth repetition ... those piercing notes went straight through my head, and I snapped.

"I opened the door to my office, and said, 'Margo, I'm trying to concentrate!' Instantly, her face fell. One moment, she was the picture of happiness, the next ... it was if I had crushed her. She stood up, closed the lid of the piano, and went upstairs without a word."

"She was very sensitive," Holly mused. "Like a bird or a butterfly."

Ardy's voice cracked. "If only I had followed her ... apologized ... said something ..." He stared at one of the Assyrian statues. "But no, like an idiot, I went back into my office to ... As if the words of a king dead for twenty-six hundred years was more important than my wife.

"I must have fallen asleep over my desk because, some while later, I was startled by a scream and a loud crash. I hurried out of my office to find—"

His voice broke, and he raised his hands to cover his eyes.

I cleared my throat. "Margo had slipped on one of the dog's tennis balls in the dark," I supplied, "and fallen down the stairs. She broke her neck—died instantly. We lived in the next house up the lane then, and when the siren of the ambulance woke me, I came over."

In my mind's eye, I could still see Margo's crumpled figure lying there at the bottom of the stairs, Ardy crouched over her sobbing, and the medics standing by helplessly.

"Since then," Ardy resumed, lowering his arms to his sides, "there has been no music in this house." His voice dropped so low as to be almost inaudible. "I would give anything to hear her voice again."

He looked at Devin. "So, you see why you must not touch the piano."

Devin nodded without speaking.

Ardy rose. "I'm going up to bed. Retire whenever you wish.

You won't disturb me."

The slender black figure made its way slowly up the stairs.

"What a sad story," Devin said, when Ardy had disappeared.

"He's always listening for her," Holly said. "He keeps the piano just as she left it."

I think the others felt the weight of sorrow as much as I did. First Holly and then Devin drifted off to their rooms, while I remained by the fire, glancing from time to time at the Steinway and the photo of Margo, and wishing that there was some comfort I could offer Ardy.

But he had never forgiven himself, and I doubted he ever would.

IT WAS AFTER MIDNIGHT, when the fire had burned out, that I finally went upstairs to bed. I never slept well in a bed other than my own, and so, despite a soft pillow and comfy mattress, I lingered in a hazy half-sleep, listening to the creaking of the old house and the occasional muffled snore from Holly in the adjacent room, and wondered if Helen was sleeping any better.

It was in this state of neither sleep nor wakefulness that I was startled by the sound of running footsteps passing my door, and a voice crying "Margo!"

I sat upright. And it was then I became aware of music. Someone was playing the piano.

"Devin, you imbecile!" I muttered, my mental cobwebs melting away.

The footsteps clattered down the stairs.

And suddenly I recognized the song—"Whither must I wander?"—and—surely it was only a memory dredged up by my awakening brain—heard a woman's voice singing those plaintive lines, especially the concluding one:

"But I go forever and come again no more."

I threw off the bedsheets and dashed out the door and around the corner to the landing at the top of the stairs, aware that the music had ceased.

"Devin!" I hissed. "What the devil are you doing?"

And there I paused.

In the moonlight slanting through the window a black shape stood poised beside the piano bench. Then it collapsed.

I raced down the stairs and dropped to my knees beside the prone form.

It wasn't Devin.

It was Ardy. His eyes were open, but his gaze was distant, as if he were looking into some place normally hidden from mortal view.

"She came," he whispered, as the light in his eyes faded and dwindled to nothing. "She came."

I laid him down and placed a cushion under his head, even as Holly called from the top of the stairs. "What's going on?"

"It's Ardy," I called back. "He's had a heart attack or something."

"I'll ring for an ambulance."

"Tell them to hurry," I said, although I knew it was too late—and even if it wasn't, I knew in my heart that Ardy wouldn't want to be brought back.

I rose, and the photograph of Margo caught my eye. I stared at it for a long moment, then retrieved my cellphone from the pocket of my jacket in the hallway.

"Caeden?" Helen's voice was slurred with sleep. "What time is it?"

"Ardy just died," I said.

"Oh dear!"

"And Helen... I'm sorry. I was thoughtless. Please come home. Take the first train in the morning. We'll get you a safer car right away..."

The doorbell rang.

"Must go," I said. "The ambulance has arrived."

ARDY LEFT NO descendants; Holly wound up his affairs and disbursed his collection.

She made no demur when I asked to be allowed to keep the photograph that had stood on the piano.

"Anything you want, Caeden. Anything at all."

"This is all I would like."

I study the photo from time to time to remind me not only of that fateful night, but of how near I came to duplicating Ardy's mistake.

I tell myself that my mind played tricks on me in the confusion and darkness. Because I knew—knew without a shadow of a doubt—that the photo was only of Margo.

But, as I looked at it in the moments after Ardy died, I was equally certain that two faces were confined in that frame.

And, if I hold it just right, with the light at the correct angle, I can still see them there.

Helen thinks I'm deluding myself.

But, as she lies beside me in bed at night, I know I'm not.

EIGHT

Hunter's Moon

A SHADOW AMONGST THE TREES … THAT'S ALL IT WAS.

A shadow cast by foliage in that mysterious time as the sun set and the full moon rose, when the last of the sun's fading golden beams yielded to shafts of cold silver, and tree-trunks and branches metamorphosed into weird, menacing forms.

Nothing moved in the woods except for the occasional squirrel and a few birds returning to their roosts.

Even so, Elder Preston, shotgun in hand, shivered as he made the rounds of his property as he did every night. He cast quick, nervous glances from side to side, unable to shake the feeling that something lurked in the gathering darkness, waiting for the moon—the Hunter's moon—to clear the treetops and dominate the sky.

There is no curse, he told himself, trying to believe the assertion. *There wasn't then, and there isn't now.*

Something dark stirred in his peripheral vision—

He halted, and with one swift motion swung his shotgun to his shoulder, and waited and watched and listened …

Fallen red and yellow leaves carpeted the ground. Neither man nor beast could move there without making noise.

"Chika!" he called, in a hushed whisper rather than the harsh, loud tone he normally used when summoning the dog. "Chika!"

His words disappeared, swallowed up by the silent forest. There was no answering patter of paws.

Muttering under his breath, he lowered his gun and

resumed his walk, arriving at the old, moss-covered stone wall that separated this swath of his woods from the orchard belonging to his neighbor. He didn't want to see her.

But there she was, the thirty-something young woman from Noo Yawk who'd come here, to the hills between Tannersville and Saugerties, and purchased the old Adamskill Farm.

Nicola Aalgaard.

Her Brooklyn accent declared her City origin in opposition to the foreignness of her name. But her looks matched it, with her short-cut blonde hair streaked with cinnamon, her dangly hoop earrings, and features that struck him as being vaguely Nordic.

She was wearing a plaid shirt and jeans and eating an apple. In her other hand she carried a basket, which she set down on the wall.

"How are you tonight, Mr. Preston?" she asked. The sharp crunch as she bit into her apple jarred his already tautly strung nerves.

"Fine," he growled.

"Care for one?" she offered, tossing her core to the ground and indicating the basket.

He dismissed the proffered fruit with a curt gesture. "No."

"Where's Chika tonight?" she inquired.

He waved his left arm in a circle. "Could be anywhere. Stupid dog broke her chain and ran off yesterday. Has she been around your place?"

She shook her head. "I'm afraid not."

Preston scowled. "I'm going to give her the thrashing of a lifetime when I catch her."

"Did you check the cave?" she suggested. "Maybe she was searching for a den."

He tensed.

"Of course," she continued, without waiting for his reply, "it would be mighty hard digging, even for a strong and determined German Shepherd, the size of some of those stones..."

The gaze she fixed on him was unnerving. Preston felt something writhe within him.

"Check her paws when you find her," she added.

He grunted, cast a glance back over his shoulder.

There...crouching in the underbrush...

He half-raised the shotgun—

"Are you sure you're all right, Mr. Preston?" she queried, regarding him with that curious gaze. "You seem awfully jittery."

"Fine, I said!"

He turned on his heel and began to walk off. He'd gone only a few steps when he swung back around.

She was watching him, with a cold light in her blue eyes, and a strange smile—half amused, half mocking—on her City-red lips.

And then, with an exaggerated motion, she rubbed her palms together crossways as if brushing dirt off them.

His chest tightened and the hand holding the shotgun trembled.

It wasn't possible!

She hadn't—she couldn't have—

"The devil take you, woman!" he yelled and pivoted away from that enigmatic, derisive smile to hurry towards his house, his refuge from the terror that, despite his best efforts to resist it, threatened to overwhelm him. She called something after him—and the words registered—but he was stumbling over fallen logs, branches plucking at his clothes and beard, scratching his cheeks, heedless of the noise he made and afraid to look up at the Hunter's moon cresting overhead—

There was no curse!

IF ONLY THE elderly Neufelds, kindred spirits—loners both—who had lived next door for decades, hadn't died without issue. In legal limbo, Adamskill Farm had lain vacant for several years—which suited Elder Preston just fine. But a historic 1852 farmhouse in the Hudson Valley was too valuable to be ignored forever. So Elder wasn't surprised when it sold to a refugee from the City desirous of escaping the congestion, noise, and pollution.

He hadn't made any effort to meet the newcomer.

But perhaps a month after the moving vans had been and gone, Chika's barking alerted him to the arrival of someone on his property.

He peered past the threadbare curtain to see a trim woman wearing a teal-colored tracksuit saunter down the long driveway, halt at the base of the steps out of range of Chika—whose barks sounded more perfunctory than aggressive—and call, "Hello! Is anyone home?"

He debated for a moment, then, annoyed by the dog's barking, grabbed his shotgun, banged the door open, and stepped out onto his porch.

"Quiet, dog!" he snapped, giving the German Shepherd a backhanded cuff. Then, "Who are you and what do you want?"

The woman cast a nervous glance at the shotgun, then replied, "I'm Nicola Aalgaard, your new neighbor at Adamskill Farm. I just thought I would introduce myself—"

"Elder Preston," he said, ignoring her outstretched hand and making no move to step down into arm's range. "Consider us introduced."

"It's very peaceful here, isn't it?" she said, lowering her hand and looking around. "Just what I've been after."

"Why?"

"I'm a writer," she said.

"Of what?"

"Ghost stories, mostly."

Preston's face darkened. "An abomination unto the Lord!"

She raised her eyebrows. "Depends whose hands they're in."

"Makes no difference." He punctuated his words with a thump of the shotgun stock on the wooden porch.

The German Shepherd whined, and he spurned it with his foot. "Enough! Lie down."

"That's a fine-looking dog," she said, as the shepherd subsided with its nose on its paws.

"Chika belonged to my late wife."

"I've always wanted a shepherd."

"Well, if you get one, keep it away from here. I'm not having any puppies."

She colored. "I wasn't implying—"

"Strong walls make for good neighbors," he added. "Good day to you." He pushed the dog out of the way of the door and went back inside. He heard her mutter something like "sanctimonious old boor" before the door banged shut.

And that, he hoped, was the end of relations with Miss Nicola Aalgaard from New York City. He put her out of his mind.

But she didn't stay there for long. Only the next week, he was sitting near Saugerties Lighthouse, watching the boats on the great Hudson River—some maritime vestige remained in his blood from his great-grandfather Chosen Preston, who'd made his money as a sea-captain before acquiring the Old Stone House and settling down—when a shadow fell across him and he looked up to see Nicola Aalgaard standing beside him.

"Mr. Preston!" she exclaimed as he rose to his feet. "Fancy meeting you here."

She was wearing a revealing designer blouse with a multicolored scarf around her neck, carrying a clipboard in her hand, and smiling.

"Taking notes for a story?" he inquired, making an effort not to look down.

Her cinnamon-blond hair bounced as she shook her head. "Collecting for victims of the earthquake in South America—"

"Let them take care of themselves," he interrupted.

"But Mr. Preston, surely you can spare—"

"It was the wrath of God upon their wickedness," he said, cutting her off. "Not any of my business."

She remained immobile with her mouth hanging open as he strode away.

He wondered what the departed Mrs. Preston—who'd gone to her eternal reward some three years ago—would have thought of this made-up young woman with a casual manner, who disdained the precepts of God. But Mrs. Preston had been too free with money for his liking. The two might have gotten on well together...

Back at home, he took out his irritation on a pile of wood that needed chopping and was fatigued when he went to bed.

Normally, he slept soundly, untroubled by conscience or the affairs of the day.

But that night, for the longest time, sleep eluded him. Eventually he took a nightcap of whisky—for purely medicinal reasons—and drifted off into slumber.

But it didn't last long. His eyes popped open, and he lay in bed wondering what had disturbed him.

He heard nothing but the normal creaks and groans of the house and the ticking of the mantle clock. And then, very faintly—

He threw back the sheets, got up, and opened the window.

The night was still, the trees standing in motionless, serried ranks beneath the glittering sky, and the harvest moon shining from behind a veil of wispy clouds. From far away came the low-pitched hoot of an owl.

That was it.

Then, as if woven into the very fabric of the night itself, came the mournful, lonely howl of a dog. It rose and fell, undulating in a way that made his flesh crawl.

"Shut up, Chika!" Preston shouted into the darkness.

The howl ceased. He waited, but it didn't recur, and he went back to bed. But he didn't sleep; he lay under the warmth of the blankets, studying the patterns in the wooden ceiling-boards, and trying to reassure himself that it had really been Chika that he'd heard . . .

IT WAS JUST OVER a week later, when Preston was making the rounds of his property, that he encountered Nicola Aalgaard again. Had he been paying more attention, he'd have avoided her; but he'd been weighing the pros and cons of performing some repairs to his house, and suddenly there she was on the other side of the boundary wall, checking the status of her apple trees.

He came to a halt with Chika, who'd been walking beside him on a short leash.

There was an awkward moment before he said, "Miss Aalgaard," and she replied with an equally civil but cool greeting.

"Is Chika always restrained?" she wondered, studying the dog. "Do you ever let her off-leash to play? I bet she'd love it."

"She doesn't need it," he said, pulling back on the leash to make Chika, who'd been trying to get her paws up on the wall to greet Nicola, to sit.

"Of course she does!"

Preston rolled his eyes. "Good heavens! Aren't you overflowing with sentimentality."

She clenched her fists. "Dogs are intelligent beings with feelings and emotions," she said stiffly. "They should be treated with love and compassion—"

He jabbed a finger in her direction. "What does the Good Book say? 'For outside are the dogs and the sorcerers and the immoral persons and the murderers and the idolaters, and everyone who loves and practices lying.'"

"It also says 'The righteous man cares for the needs of his animal,'" she retorted, her blue eyes blazing.

"Don't quote Scripture to me!" he shot back. "She gets food and water and shelter. That's enough."

"Hardly!"

"That's what the law says," he replied. "And I'm a man of the law." He gave Chika's leash a sharp jerk. "Let's go."

Chika kept looking back, forcing him to correct her. He was glad when he was out of Nicola Aalgaard's sight. She was nothing but trouble.

He saw nothing more of her for several days.

It was purely by chance that he noticed her one morning, and only because she was wearing a red jacket that stood out vividly against the fading foliage on the hillside that rose up behind their properties. From his back porch, he watched her through binoculars as she climbed the slope and crisscrossed it, going from one rocky outcropping to another, getting ever closer to . . .

With an imprecation, he threw down the binoculars, pulled on his boots, grabbed his shotgun, and unhooked Chika, then tramped across the neglected north field, Chika slinking behind, until he reached the base of the hill.

He hadn't come here in years, and there was no path, but he knew the way well enough. Motioning for Chika to follow him, he began the ascent.

She wrote ghost stories, did she? If she wanted a fright, he'd give her one.

From time to time he glimpsed the red of her jacket above him, and then it disappeared behind a protruding angle of rock.

Placing his feet as quietly as he could, he crept past a tangle of roots until he was able to peer around the edge of the outcropping. She was there, kneeling on the ground, studying the blocked-up entrance of a small cave. Her right index finger traced the outline of a faint, weatherworn cross on one of the stones.

Grinning, he raised the shotgun to his shoulder, pointed it into the sky and pulled the trigger.

She screamed, spun around, lost her balance, and fell onto her side.

"Good thing you weren't a Redcoat and me a Minuteman," Preston laughed unpleasantly as the echoes of the deafening blast faded. "Wouldn't have been much left of you."

She scrambled to her feet, dusting herself off and glaring fury at him. "What do you think you're doing? You could have killed me!"

"'Thou shalt not commit murder,'" Preston said. "It says nothing about scaring the pants off someone."

"That was not very neighborly," she gritted.

"Neither is trespassing," Preston responded.

She blushed. "It was accidental. I—"

"You what? Are you a spelunker as well as a writer?"

She straightened, took a deep breath. "Actually, yes. Almost. I collect minerals and crystals."

She looked away from him, at the cave. "Did you know this was here?"

"Of course. I know every inch of my land."

"Why is it blocked up? Is there ... is there anything in there?"

"Many, many years ago," Preston said. "My great-grandfather had a dog that died. He buried it in there."

"Oh," she said, sounding disappointed.

"Did you want a ghost story? Some grisly legend about witches' covens or demons stalking the hills? Strange beasts?

Grist for your distorted imagination?"

She stiffened. "I'm sorry I intruded—"

"Get away from there!" Preston yelled suddenly.

Chika, who had been pawing at the rocks, slunk away.

Preston returned his attention to the woman. "I would appreciate it if you would stay off my property."

She bit her lip, nodded silently, then began to clamber back down the hillside.

Preston waited until she was out of sight. Then he checked to make sure the rocks blocking the cave were still tightly in place.

And with a shudder he made his way home, Chika trailing disconsolately behind.

The day passed all too quickly for his liking. He feared the dream would come that night and it did, as it had since childhood, when he'd first seen the cave and his father had told him the story . . .

He was walking through the woods at night, slipping easily between the trunks, in that strange unreality of dreams. He was alone. No, not alone. Someone was with him. Three someones. Without seeing their faces, for they were mere pale outlines, he knew them to be his great-grandfather, Chosen Preston, and Chosen's two older sons, Elect and Assured, Elder's great-great-uncles.

Elder had never met them, of course, as they had died long before he was born. But he'd seen faded, sepia-colored photographs.

They were climbing a hillside, scrambling over rocky outcroppings in the distorted light of a dull, gray moon. Something howled in the distance, a weird, unearthly cry.

They came to a cave, its entrance blocked by stones, with a cross carved in the center one.

As they stood there, the stones began to tumble down of

their own accord. Elder wanted to run, but something held him fast, his dream-feet planted to the ground.

One by one, the stones toppled, exposing a black cavity.

And in the cavity, something blacker than night, blacker than space, watched them with baleful eyes that glowed like burning coals, yet were as frigid as the emptiness between the stars.

The last stone dropped and the darkness erupted, swallowing Chosen and his two sons—

Elder awoke, gasping, and shivering with sweat. With a shaking hand he reached for the bottle beside his bed and took a long drink. Then another. And a third.

For the remainder of the night he lay there, waiting for morning to arrive.

IT WAS ABOUT two weeks after the encounter on the hillside, when Elder Preston was shopping in Saugerties, that he saw Nicola Aalgaard emerge from a second-hand bookstore tucked away in an old building on a quiet side-street. When she'd vanished, he hurried over and entered the repository, easing carefully between teetering stacks of disintegrating volumes that smelled of age and mold, until he reached the desk in the back.

"Why, Mr. Preston!" exclaimed the proprietress, a middle-aged woman who also served on the board of the Saugerties Historical Society. "What a coincidence! I was just thinking of you, because I received this collection of—"

Preston tapped a finger on the desk. "The woman who was just in here—"

The proprietress blinked. "Miss Aalgaard, yes."

"What did she want?"

"She was looking for information on local legends."

"What did you tell her?"

"Nothing much. I pointed her in the direction of some of the books . . ." She indicated a shelf labelled Local History and Folklore. "She bought a couple."

"Did one of them happen to include the story of Chosen Preston?"

She rubbed her chin. "It's possible that one of them might have mentioned the Preston Curse. I don't know for certain."

He smacked his hand down on the desk.

"Did you know she's my neighbor? That's all I need, having her head filled with an old legend."

"Even if it's true?" she replied.

He brought his other hand sharply down onto the desk and leaned towards her, breathing heavily. "It's not true! It's not!"

She pushed her chair back.

"There's no need to get upset, Mr. Preston. Now, wouldn't you like to look at—"

"No!" he spat. "I wouldn't."

He stormed out, sending one of the stacks of books crashing to the floor.

His anger had subsided somewhat by the time he returned to OldStone House. So what if Nicola Aalgaard read about the legend? He'd warned her to keep off his property. Surely she wouldn't dare go to the cave again, not after the way he'd scared her . . .

But, another voice in his mind countered, what if she did? What if he had angered her more than frightened her?

What would it matter?

There was no curse!

He forced his thoughts into other channels. And yet, day by day, his anxiety increased. He scrutinized the hillside for hours at a time and, each night, watched with deepening misgiving the moon as it waxed inexorably towards fullness.

The hunter's moon.

And then Chika disappeared. She'd been there in the morning, when he'd fed her. She'd been there in the early afternoon when he'd yelled at her for barking at birds.

But now, when he brought her bowl again, she'd vanished, leaving behind a length of broken chain.

He paced around his living room, pausing every so often to peer out the window, checking the porch where Chika used to lie, in case she had returned. Stupid dog.

Should he go and look for her?

She could be anywhere. Over at Nicola Aalgaard's most likely, getting fawned over and petted.

Or possibly—

No. He wasn't climbing the hillside. Not now. Even though it was only a legend.

To be sure, Great-grandfather Chosen Preston had been a hard man, harsh to both man and beast—unforgiving to his neighbors, and not sparing the whip on his horses.

Family history recorded that he'd owned a black hound, which he'd abused mercilessly until one day the formerly docile creature, tormented beyond endurance, turned on him, and Chosen, a strong man, strangled it with his bare hands.

And local records confirmed that, at about the same time, he'd whipped one of his servants so badly for a trivial offense that the man had nearly died and remained crippled forever. His wife, a "peculiar woman," had hated Chosen ever after. And, it was claimed, cursed him—and his family. Who treats a man like a dog shall die by a dog, she'd intoned.

No one doubted that Elect and Assured had been cut from the same cloth as their father. And all three had been found dead on the night of the hunter's moon, years apart, but each with his face frozen in terror.

But Elder's grandfather—the youngest of the three brothers—had died of old age. And Elder's father had collapsed of a heart attack while fishing.

There was no curse!

His shotgun was leaning against the wall by the door. He'd make his rounds before dark and be safely home before the moon rose. Chika had probably run off after a squirrel and was stuck in the forest, her chain caught on a branch. Serve her right.

And so, he walked the route he'd walked thousands of times before, every now and then calling Chika's name and telling himself, as the sun dipped towards the horizon, that he had nothing to worry about.

He'd lived seventy years without incident. This hunter's moon was no different from any of the preceding ones.

So he said—until he met Nicola Aalgaard standing beside the wall wiping dust off her hands...

HIS HOME... he had to make it home... bar the door... shutter the windows... turn on all the lights...

Dread bordering on panic overwhelmed him as he ran, stumbling and lurching through the rapidly darkening woods, while the shadows lengthened and reached out like a myriad blindly grasping limbs.

Who treats a man like a dog shall die by a dog.

Nonsense! What were the angry words of a peculiar woman uttered so long ago?

There was no curse!

There was no phantom black dog!

Chosen had died in his study from apoplexy, not fright.

Elect had simply fallen in the woods and broken his neck, the ghastly expression on his face notwithstanding.

And Assured—he'd probably drunk bad liquor, that was why he looked as though he'd gazed into the pit of Hell.

It was purely coincidence that each had died on a hunter's

moon—nothing else.

Preston's breath rasped in his throat.

Not far now . . .

And the business about the local minister declaring himself powerless and a priest being called to deal with it . . .

More nonsense.

The Papists were only one step removed from the devil, themselves.

There was nothing but dust in that cave, dust and the skeleton of Chosen's long-dead hound.

Bones. Dry bones.

And it was the wind, or Chika, that howled on the night of the full moon, not a creature of darkness hungering to be set free . . .

"Deliver my life from the power of the dog!" he gasped as he ran. "Have mercy on your elect!"

His heart pounded as though it would burst, and the vise tightened around his chest, and pain lanced down his left arm. But it would pass, as it always had before.

There! Ahead of him, warm light shining from the windows of Old Stone House.

He staggered and looked back—

—as a bounding blackness surged out of the woods and the moonlight, covering the ground faster than any normal creature could run. Darker than night, yet somehow it glowed or shimmered—

His shotgun roared again and again, the blasts having no effect on the racing shadow. It leaped towards him and he thought he glimpsed fangs and claws and chilling eyes—

He screamed, dropped his gun, and threw up his arms, even as his legs gave way beneath him, but it was the words that Nicola Aalgaard had shouted after him that flashed through his mind as his final conscious thought—

He shall have judgment without mercy who has shown no mercy.

Then blackness engulfed him, and stillness returned to the night.

FAR UP ON THE hillside, in front of a blocked-up cave marked with a cross, Chika turned her muzzle skyward and bayed at the hunter's moon.

NINE

Kibble in the Marmalade

MRS. MORRISON WAS TOO BUSY TO DIE.

And so, she didn't.

At least not completely.

Mrs. Morrison, I should explain, had been "in service" at the ancestral home—Overton Hall, located not far from Salisbury—for decades. Generations, actually. She had initially been employed as a young woman by my paternal grandparents, served my parents, and then remained when Phyllis and I inherited the Hall.

By now she was positively ancient—pushing one hundred—yet she remained a dynamo, a diminutive, withered, but vigorous-in-spirit woman; one, moreover, who refused all the offers of a comfortable retirement which Phyllis and I proposed to her.

"Don't be silly, my dears," she said, in her squeaky, high-pitched voice, her blue eyes twinkling beneath her shock of white hair. "Whatever would I do?"

"Read," Phyllis suggested, leaning close and shouting in order to make herself heard over the shriek of Mrs. Morrison's ineffective hearing aide. "Listen to music, take up painting . . ."

Mrs. Morrison laughed and rubbed her knobby hands on her well-worn and stained apron, which I had no doubt rivalled her for age. "What a silly notion! I don't have any hobbies. Taking care of you and Aaron is my life."

"But you've earned it!"

"Stuff and nonsense," she cackled, shuffling off. "Stuff and nonsense!"

Well, what could we do but smile at each other, hire extra day help for the heavier chores—gritting our teeth at the additional expense—and allow Mrs. Morrison to continue puttering around making tea, baking scones, and preparing the occasional breakfast? And if the tea was too strong, the scones dry, and the bacon overdone—we knew they were made with love.

Truth to tell, we enjoyed her presence, as she was a link to the past, to the days when Overton Hall had truly been a genteel, stately house and not, as now, a slightly run-down home which we had difficulty maintaining, thanks to a sluggish economy and ever-increasing taxes.

But, of course, it couldn't last forever, and one day Mrs. Morrison didn't put in an appearance from the bed-sitting room she occupied in the east wing. I'd gone to work early, and Phyllis phoned to tell me that she'd found Mrs. Morrison dead in her bed.

I could hardly believe it. "I almost imagined she'd outlive us," I said.

"So did I," Phyllis replied sadly. "It won't be the same without her."

And it wasn't.

We arranged a nice funeral and saw Mrs. Morrison laid to rest in the family plot near my parents and grandparents, whom she had so faithfully served and who could never have managed without her.

At the time, we were experiencing a particularly difficult period, and, forced to economize, made the decision to discharge the day help and take on all the domestic chores ourselves. Since we both tended to work long hours at our tedious but not particularly well-paying jobs, we'd get up early in order to set the table, make the bed, run the dishwasher, and prepare the dogs' dinner before leaving for work, so that when we returned home exhausted, there'd be less to do before bed.

For a week or so, all went according to plan, the routine becoming almost second nature.

It was then that the haunting—for such we now know it to have been—began.

I came home late from work one day to find Phyllis in a sour mood.

"Bad day?" I asked, when the usual greeting kiss failed to materialize.

"You could at least have set the table and gotten the dogs' dinners ready before you left," she said, transfixing me with one of those icy stares that are the bane and dread of every husband's existence.

"But I did!" I protested.

She grabbed me by the arm and hauled me into the dining room. "You call this set?"

I stared at the table in confusion. Knives and forks lay in a jumbled heap, the glasses were overturned, the salt and pepper containers were spilling their contents, and a vase of flowers lay on its side, a water-stain spreading over the lace tablecloth.

"Maybe one of the dogs knocked into the table or pulled on the tablecloth," I said. "It was set when I left."

She regarded me skeptically. "Seriously, Aaron?" she said witheringly. "They've never done anything like that before."

I fetched a clean tablecloth and re-laid the setting while Phyllis cooked. We ate in chilly silence.

The next day it was I who returned home first to find dirty dishes scattered all over the kitchen.

When I pointed this out to Phyllis, she said. "That's a low blow, Aaron. They were loaded in the dishwasher and set to go."

"What? You think that I took them out?"

"Well, they didn't climb out on their own."

"Maybe you just forgot to load it," I replied intemperately.

I spent the rest of the night in the dog house.

The next day, it was dirty laundry strewn up and down the stairs, even though we were both sure the basket had been left in the laundry room. The day after that, the bed was torn to pieces and another round of mutual accusation ensued, with the dogs coming in for heavy suspicion.

But then we began to wonder.

"This doesn't make sense," Phyllis said, as we remade the bed. "It's as if somebody is coming in here and deliberately messing up the house."

"What reason could anyone have?" I replied. "Besides, the alarm system hasn't been triggered, and even if they bypassed it, there are the dogs to contend with."

Morgan and Mordred. Two Dobermans not noted for friendliness towards uninvited strangers.

I rubbed my chin. "Not unless..."

"Unless what?" Phyllis demanded, punching a pillow with unnecessary vigor.

"We have a poltergeist."

She stared at me in disbelief for a moment before mashing the pillow onto the bed. "Have you gone and lost it?"

"Can you think of a better explanation?" I countered, fluffing my own pillow. "If I'm not doing it, and you're not doing it, and the dogs are innocent, and there's no intruder..."

"Is Overton Hall haunted?" she asked pointedly, yanking the sheets towards her side.

"I've never heard of any supernatural presence," I replied, scratching my head.

"Then let's try to think of a more normal explanation," Phyllis said. "I'm not buying the ghost theory."

There spoke my rational wife.

And we tried, racking our brains. But we couldn't come up with a reasonable explanation.

In the meantime, the disorder continued. Keys placed in one

location turned up in another. Shoes neatly lined up became obstacle courses for us to stumble over in the dark. Coats vanished from the closet and migrated to the pantry. Letters and envelopes left neatly on the kitchen counter or my desk made their way under the sofas. The television remote was discovered in the freezer, the dogs' bowls in the clothes washer. Books in the bathtub. Underwear in the china closet. Soap in with the teabags.

That was the last straw.

"We have a poltergeist," Phyllis said in disgust, dumping the undrinkable brew down the drain. "I told you so."

"Then let's get rid of it," I proclaimed, deciding that the better part of valor was to summon professional help.

I called for the local vicar, who came and prayed over each room of the house.

The disturbances continued.

On to Plan B and following.

We lit candles. Burned incense. Recited incantations. Hung up religious pictures.

All to no avail.

Cheese in the postbox. Kibble in the marmalade. Phyllis's engagement ring in a bottle of pills.

My nerves in tatters.

We were at our wits' end.

We looked morosely at each other over breakfast one day.

"I don't know what to do," Phyllis sighed, collecting the dishes together, "short of hiring an exorcist—I hear the Catholics know a thing or two about it. It's been a nightmare ever since Mrs. Morrison died. It's all her fault for popping off and leaving us."

"Blaming a centenarian for leaving this mortal coil is hardly fair," I protested. "Don't you think she was due for some eternal reward?"

"Due, yes," Phyllis said. "But desirous . . . I wonder. She was the working type, not the kind to sit on a cloud playing a harp 24/7."

That sounded pretty boring to me, too.

"But . . ." I said, "you're not suggesting that Mrs. Morrison is haunting us, are you? My family loved her. You and I loved her. Besides, she's just the opposite of this poltergeist. She reduced entropy, she didn't increase it."

"I wasn't insinuating anything," Phyllis replied. "I was just commenting on the time frame."

Suddenly, (I don't know why since I'm not prone to them) a flash of insight burst upon me.

"Forget the dishes!" I cried, jumping to my feet and halting Phyllis, who was about to carry them out to the kitchen.

"What?" she goggled.

"Just leave them," I said. "Let's see what happens."

She looked at me as if I'd suddenly gone insane, then set the dishes down again with a clatter.

"I've never seen dishes wash themselves," she said acidly. "But if you want to eat off filthy plates, fine."

I could hardly wait to return home from work that evening. As it happened, Phyllis and I arrived within seconds of each other.

"The moment of truth," I said, inserting my key into the lock and opening the door. Morgan and Mordred met us, wagging their tails.

I flicked on the light. Our slippers were lined up neatly on the mat, our housecoats hung on their rack.

We entered the dining room. Phyllis stared in amazement. The table was set, and there wasn't a dirty dish in sight.

"You came home from work at lunchtime!" Phyllis laughed, poking me in the ribs.

"I never left the office," I replied. "You can check with my staff."

"Then you hired a housekeeper without telling me!"

"Not that, either."

"Well, it couldn't have been the poltergeist."

"It was," I grinned.

"But the house is immaculate!"

"And who always kept it that way?"

She stared at me in puzzlement. "Mrs. Morrison?"

"Right in one."

"But then why make all the mess? Why behave like a poltergeist?"

"To get our attention," I explained excitedly, holding up one finger after another, "and to make us miss her. To have us stop doing the work ourselves, because if we left everything neat and tidy, what was there for her to do?"

Phyllis's face was a study in conflicted emotions. "A ghost wanting a job?" she said dubiously.

"Even a ghost likes to feel needed," I said. I put my arm around Phyllis's shoulder. "Isn't it great to have her back?"

From then on, we left the dirty dishes on the table, the laundry on the floor, the bed unmade, the rooms in a mess.

And when we returned home each day, the house would be spick and span, the bed made, the table set for dinner, and everything in its allotted place.

As I said, Mrs. Morrison was too busy to die.

TEN

The Quarry Gardens

IT WAS LATE AFTERNOON WHEN I SAW HER.

The surface of the water was a tranquil tapestry of reflections—the lush green of cypresses, the red of bottle brushes, the yellow of black-eyed susans, the pink of oleanders—all set in vivid contrast to the browns and grays of the high walls of the old limestone quarry. Once, it had been a scar on the landscape—an ugly chasm carved out as a source of material for highway construction and then abandoned, to be taken over by weeds and brush and muck and dark, depressing puddles of stagnant water.

I remembered it as a place we boys would sneak to on a dare, defying our parents' prohibitions. In search of excitement and heedless of danger, we'd clamber down the crumbling walls into the spooky depths. Perhaps, if we were lucky, we'd find a shark's tooth or a fragment of fossilized dugong bone and return home to our oblivious parents with no more than a scraped knee or torn fingernail to show for our foolhardiness.

But now, decades later, the quarry was a jewel. It had been purchased by a philanthropist, who had painstakingly and lovingly transformed it into a botanical garden. The walls had been terraced, and now azaleas and roses flourished in hanging gardens. Islands linked by bridges rose above the flooded floor, and supported palm trees and clumps of bamboo. Waterfalls plummeted from the brink, while fountains sprayed silver plumes of clear water into the fragrant air.

It was a lovely spot, and I often came to amble along the trails, seeking out some blossom I'd never seen before. Sometimes I'd simply sit on a bench and enjoy the panorama and listen to the cascades and the birds. Other times, like today, I'd focus on the waters, studying the reflections that glimmered like masterpieces of Impressionist art, admiring the ripples made by the breeze, trying to catch a glimpse of the koi and giant catfish and grass carp that inhabited the deeper parts.

And yet, there was another reason that I came.

I often wondered if I would see her.

Angelique.

But in ten years' time I never had. I'd spot a fish, or a turtle, or the shadow of a bird flying overhead. But never her.

Never Angelique.

And really, it was silly of me to imagine that I would. Such things were for stories; they didn't happen in real life.

I'd visited her grave in the cemetery of the little white-washed Baptist church a mile or two down the road, and laid flowers beside her tombstone. But I wondered if that was enough. I wondered if she knew.

And so, whenever I visited the quarry gardens, it was with a mixture of hope and trepidation. Because, if by some miracle she did appear, then what?

I arrived at a stone bench situated on a little promontory on the lower level, only a few feet above the waterline, and there I sat, leaning over the water's edge so that I could gaze at the reflections and into the depths.

"Pray for her soul," Father Pietro had counselled me, back when she died. "That's all you can do now."

And so I did, every time.

"And for your own," he'd added sternly, once I'd confessed.

And I did that too.

A flicker of movement in the water caught my attention. I stared, trying to determine what had caused it.

And as I attempted to focus my eyes on the subtly shifting reflections, her face rose up from the shadowed deeps to float, it seemed, just below the surface. Her hazel eyes regarded me steadily, and her hair, of a shade somewhere between brown and blonde, splayed out like a penumbra around her pale face. Her lips formed a straight line beneath her celestial-shaped nose, giving no hint of the engaging smile she had been wont to bestow on friend and stranger alike.

My heart lurched and I slid off the bench onto my knees, stretching out a hand, then halting the movement with my fingertips scarcely above the water's surface.

"Angelique," I whispered. "I'm sorry. I'm so very, very sorry."

For a moment, the lips parted in a smile—gentle, forgiving—and then a voice from behind me said,

"Did you drop something?"

I started, and, the moment broken, her eyes were only lily pads, her hair a dead palm branch in the tree behind me and her lips a blooming bottle brush.

I clambered to my feet, to find a gardener standing beside me. He must have been about seventy. His face was sun-lined and his chin stubbly. He wore a faded tee shirt, jeans, and a baseball cap with an unidentifiable logo. He carried a shovel over his shoulder.

"No," I replied. "Just looking."

He leaned his shovel against the trunk of the palm tree.

"You're mighty pale. Look like you've just seen a ghost."

I subsided back onto the bench. I felt as if I had, too.

"Must be the heat," I said.

The gardener removed his cap and scratched his head before putting the cap back on. "It wouldn't surprise me if there were ghosts here," he said conversationally. "People have died here, you know."

"Is that so?" I asked, my mind still whirling from what I thought I'd seen.

He pulled a packet of gum from his pocket, offered me a stick (which I declined), then unwrapped one, popped it into his mouth, and began to chew.

"The last one was a girl," he said. "Young woman, really. I reckon it was about ten years ago, give or take. Do you want to hear the story?"

He didn't wait for me to say that I already knew it. "There was a pastor down the road," he said, making a vague motion roughly in the direction of the little church. "He was a married man with a couple of kids, a boy and a girl, twins about eleven or twelve. This young woman—I can't think of her name—belonged to his church. She was quite attractive, so I understand, and a good deal younger than him. She was from out of state—up north somewhere.

"There was some kind of attraction between them, and you can guess what happened. The pastor divorced his wife and about six months later married the new girl. His ex-wife moved out west. It caused quite a stir—back then, in a small town, where everyone knew everyone else, things like that didn't go over very well. You'd think that the pastor would have shouldered most of the blame, but that wasn't the case. People saw this middle-aged fellow—and a man of God to boot—being bewitched by a pretty young woman. They were willing to give him a bye while foisting the blame for the break-up of the marriage on her."

"Not fair," I said.

"Not at all," he replied. "Apparently she was taken completely by surprise. I guess she never thought that people would turn on her the way they did. They shunned her. They'd look away when she was walking down the street, refuse to talk to her, wouldn't sit next to her in church. I don't know what they were like at home, but even the pastor's kids ignored her in public."

"It must have been tough," I said.

The gardener nodded. "Tough isn't the word for it. But it continued for years, until the twins went off to college. One evening the woman went for a walk, like she always did. But that night, she never came home. The sheriff thought maybe she'd skipped town, but a few days later they found her here, floating at the bottom of the quarry. Right over there."

He pointed to an inlet only a few feet away. My eyes travelled up the nearly vertical face of the quarry wall. A terrible to place to die.

"Did she fall in accidentally in the dark," the gardener continued, "or did she jump because she couldn't take it anymore?" He shrugged. "Either way, it was a shame."

"A great shame," I replied.

"So, if she was a suicide, it wouldn't surprise me if her ghost haunted the quarry," he said. He gave a short, mirthless laugh. "But I don't come here at night to find out."

He reached for another piece of gum. "The pastor left town soon afterwards. Never did hear where he went."

"There's more to the story," I said quietly, thinking that I needed to defend Angelique.

"You've heard about it?" he exclaimed, sounding irritated.

I nodded. "I used to know all of them—the pastor, Collette, and Angelique. That was her name. I didn't attend their church, but I took care of them periodically as their dentist, both before and after the divorce and remarriage. I ran into Collette about five years after Angelique died. She'd come back to town to clear up some business affairs. We ended up talking about old times, and she told me what had really happened."

"Which was what?" the gardener asked, leaning on the back of the bench and chewing hard.

"Well, it seems that Collette had never wanted to get married in the first place but had been pushed into it by her parents. She never loved the pastor. In fact, she'd never been attracted to men at all—just the opposite."

He whistled.

"The pastor didn't divorce her—she left him to go and live with another woman. She abandoned him and the children. He was crushed. He turned to Angelique—not just for himself, but because he needed someone to mother the twins."

I sighed. "People around here can be pretty harsh. The pastor never wanted anyone—let alone his children—to know the real reason why their mom had left."

The gardener hitched up his jeans. "So the girl—Angelique—kept her mouth shut for the sake of the kids? So they wouldn't get picked on by other kids?"

I nodded. "She never said a word. Kept it all a secret."

"Well, that beats everything," he said.

"Angelique wasn't a home-wrecker at all," I said. "But everyone thought she was."

Myself included, I added silently, thinking how tired and worn-looking she'd become, how lifeless and dispirited. For I too had been one of the sanctimonious, holier-than-thou multitude who had misjudged, condemned, and shunned her ... and possibly driven her to take—intentionally or not—her own life. I hadn't literally picked up a stone, but I might just as well have.

"That's pretty sad," the gardener said. He glanced at his watch, then picked up his shovel. "I must be going. Enjoy the rest of your visit."

"Thank you," I said, as he ambled away.

I rose and stared into the water again. But clouds had drifted across the face of the sun and there was nothing to see but a featureless, blue-gray expanse.

And yet, as I ascended the steps leading out of the quarry,

passing between mounds of azaleas in full bloom, I felt a sense of peace, as if my prayers had, after all, been finally answered.

ELEVEN

Meadow Mist

ANNIE CRACKED OPEN THE WOODEN DOOR OF the old farmhouse and looked out. A layer of mist drifted above the ground, blanketing the fields and wrapping around the trunks of the trees. The hills, draped with gossamer shrouds, lay like bodies covered with burial cloths, reminding her of that awful day in childhood when her three younger siblings had died of diphtheria in the span of forty-eight hours. The sun, barely peeping above the horizon, shot translucent beams across the landscape, and sparkled in the heavy dew that weighed down the grass.

The air was still, but not silent. A cow lowed in the distance, while a blue jay jeered from a stand of oak trees. A small stream chuckled down from the ridge behind the house before crossing the meadow and winding down the valley.

She inhaled the fresh scent of the morning, filling her lungs and wishing she could fill her soul.

Once upon a time, she could have; and perhaps other people could sense the almost mystical tranquility of this place, a peacefulness that she had once enjoyed here.

But years ago, that peace had been shattered forever. She shivered and reached for her red plaid shawl hung on a hook beside the door to drape it across her shoulders.

"You aren't going out now, are you?" her daughter, Rebecca, asked, emerging from her bedroom to stand behind her. "You'll catch cold."

Annie shrugged. "So what if I do? It's the day."

"Don't go out, Gramma," a young voice pleaded, accompanying the words with a tug on her skirt. "Please."

"It's all right, chicken," Annie said, bending over to ruffle the hair of a little girl of six or seven. "Gramma will be fine."

Rebecca exhaled loudly and spoke with exasperation in her voice. "It's been thirty years that you've been going out there. You must have covered every inch of that ground."

"Yes, Annie," said a man's voice. Rebecca's husband, Kirby, rubbed sleep from his eyes. "What's the point? Jackson is gone."

"Not to me, he's not," Annie said stubbornly, swinging around to face them. "Not to me. One day I'll find him."

Rebecca and Kirby exchanged helpless glances.

Annie scowled. "I'm an old woman. The least you can do is humor me."

"You're not that old," Rebecca said.

"I'm fifty. That's old enough."

Rebecca shrugged. "Suit yourself then. Be foolish."

"Love is not foolish," Annie snapped.

"But clinging to the past is."

"Ladies!" Kirby began, "there's no need to fight—"

Annie ignored him, staring instead at Rebecca. "He was your father, don't forget."

Rebecca flushed. "I was two years old. It's not as though I ever knew him."

Annie raised her hand as if to slap her, then lowered it and sighed. "I suppose not. You don't know what it is to lose half of yourself. To be widowed at twenty..."

"Let her go, Rebecca," Kirby said, more softly this time. He laid his arm across his wife's shoulders. "I expect that in her place I might do the same."

Rebecca shrugged free and turned aside. "Suit yourself then."

Annie bent over to kiss the little girl on the top of her head.

"Be good, punkin'. When I get back, we'll make a Jefferson Davis pie. Would you like that?"

"Yes, Gramma."

"Good."

Annie cinched her shawl tighter. Kirby held the door open for her and she stepped outside.

Her booted feet left tracks in the wet grass as she headed across the meadow, and the dense mist embraced her.

1864. A year she would never forget until her dying day. What had it been like for her people, she wondered, outnumbered and outgunned by Yankee invaders?

Perhaps it had been misty, like now. Or perhaps the sun had shone brightly over a day that would have been beautiful, otherwise.

She didn't know, because she and two-year-old Rebecca had fled days earlier from the path of the colliding forces. Far enough away to be safe, but not so far as to escape the faint sound of distant gunfire. She'd sheltered with a number of other women in the cellars of an abandoned farmhouse . . . and had stayed there for several days, until a messenger brought word that, although the Confederates had retreated and the Union troops hadn't pressed their advantage, it was still too dangerous to return home. She'd made her way to Charlottesville and stayed with her sister until the North had finished ravaging the South and Lee surrendered the broken, exhausted remnants of the Army of Northern Virginia at Appomattox.

Then she'd returned home . . . to what was left of it.

The house still stood, but bullet holes riddled the walls and shattered windows looked out over fields trampled by horses into quagmires rutted by wagons and caissons. The fences had collapsed, the chicken coop lay in ruins . . . not that there were any chickens or livestock left . . .

And the meadow . . .

The meadow was dotted with mounds and turned earth where the fallen had been hastily buried where they lay.

She repaired what she could while waiting for Jackson. She hung new curtains, prepared the house for his homecoming, which surely would be any day.

The grass grew back. Flowers bloomed in the meadow. But there was no sign of Jackson.

Finally, she learned from a returning soldier—a neighbor—that Jackson had perished in that encounter.

Where had it happened? He didn't know, exactly.

Where was Jackson buried? He didn't know that, either. Everything had happened so quickly ... there hadn't been time to think, to mourn ...

But Jackson lay here, somewhere, among so many others ...

Had she not had a child to care for, she would have allowed grief to claim her.

Then, a year to the day after the battle, she had been out in the meadow picking flowers, just after sunrise, when suddenly cannon and gunfire and the shouts and cries of fighting and dying men assailed her ears. Frozen, then panicked, she'd swung in a circle, expecting to see troops of soldiers in blue and grey locked in deadly combat.

Had the war resumed?

Had—somehow—the Confederacy risen again?

But there was nothing. Only the meadow, the fields, the hills, the forest. The light of dawn bluing the sky.

She sank to the ground.

Echoes. She was hearing echoes.

And lost among those faint reverberations from the past, must be Jackson's. His last words. His final cry.

She longed to hear them.

But the sounds faded and she was left with only her own sobs.

The years passed. She struggled alone to run the farm and raise Rebecca, until Kirby married her and assumed responsibility for both.

Every year, on the anniversary of the battle, she went out into the meadow and listened, hoping against hope to hear a familiar voice amidst the clamor of war... to find where he lay, forgotten, unremembered and unlamented, except by her.

No one else could hear the yells, the shouts, the screams... She had learned that. No one but her.

And each year they became a little fainter, a little less distinct. And each year her hope faded a little more.

Rebecca was right. It was cool today. The sun, unwontedly weak, seemed unable to dispel the mist, which condensed into a light drizzle. Her shawl became heavy with damp, and moisture seeped into her boots. All day long, as the hours came and went, she crisscrossed the meadow, the mounds now nearly flattened out by the passage of time.

Kirby brought her a cup of hot tea, which she accepted gratefully before sending him back to the house, his pleas for her to return rebuffed. Still she persisted, listening, always listening, searching for that one voice that she would know above all others.

The mist thickened, becoming gray in the dwindling light of the afternoon, standing in thick pillars between the trees and moving in swirls and billows across the meadow—as if was both dead and yet alive.

Chills shook her and her steps became leaden, her wet clothes weighed her down. Fatigue threatened to end her quest, to force her to admit defeat, as she had so many times before.

But then, at the farthest end of the meadow, where the forest was encroaching and black walnut and hickory trees straddled the creek, she paused, head tilted to one side.

Amidst the faint cries and moans and gunshots and clash of

swords and bayonets—surely that was his voice—!

And standing there, beside the creek, almost as insubstantial as the mist itself, she glimpsed a figure in Confederate grey, arms extended—

"Jackson!" she cried, flinging herself forwards into the mist. "Jackson!"

"**SHE SHOULD BE BACK** by now," Rebecca said, peering out of the window into a dense grey-white void. "Twilight's coming, and it's almost time for supper!"

"Gramma promised to make a pie!" the little girl cried.

"I know, darling," Rebecca said.

Kirby threw another log onto the fire. "I'll go and look for her." He reached for his coat.

"I'll come with you," Rebecca said.

"There's no need—"

"Two of us will be faster," she said, putting on her own garment. "Stay here and play with your dolls," she instructed the little girl. "Daddy and I will be back soon."

"Annie was in the lower meadow earlier," Kirby said, as they stepped outside. "So let's begin in the upper."

Rebecca nodded as they headed away from the house. "How could she spend all day out in this? You can't see more than two or three feet ahead!"

"She's a determined woman," Kirby replied. "Very determined."

He pointed. "Why don't you take that side of the creek, and I'll take the other."

Rebecca hesitated. "No . . . we could get disoriented. Let's stay together."

Kirby gave her a questioning look. "As long as you can hear the creek—"

"I want to stay together!"

Kirby shrugged. "As you wish."

"Mother!" Rebecca called. "Where are you? Mother!"

But if there was an answer, it was swallowed up by the cloying mist.

It took an hour before they found her, and then it was Kirby who spotted a splash of red near a thicket during a momentary thinning of the mist.

"Mother!" Rebecca cried, dashing ahead and dropping to her knees beside the prone figure.

Annie lay sprawled across a low mound at the base of a hickory tree, its branches outspread. Her face was pressed to the wet ground.

Kirby crouched down, touched a cold cheek, and then carefully rolled her over. Annie's eyes gazed sightlessly heavenward, and Kirby gently closed them.

"No," Rebecca sobbed. "She can't be ..."

"What's this?" Kirby asked, indicating a chain dangling from Annie's clenched right hand. He pried her stiff fingers open and exposed a round object.

Rebecca wiped it against her skirt, revealing the golden sheen of brass. She studied the image of a mounted man cutting a cloak with a sword. "It's Saint Martin of Tours. A patron saint of soldiers."

"Have you ever seen it before?" Kirby asked.

"Never. And I know all of mother's jewelry. I'm sure this isn't hers."

"Then where did it come from?" Kirby wondered, looking around. "It couldn't just have been lying here ... and the ground hasn't been disturbed ..."

Rebecca turned it over. "There are initials—J.F.D. Jackson Frederick Doyle," she whispered. "I can't believe it. She found him. After all these years. She found him."

"Let's take her home," Kirby said, positioning himself to lift Annie's limp form.

"No," Rebecca said. "She belongs here."

She raised the medallion to her lips, then placed it back in her mother's hand and closed the cold fingers over it.

TWELVE
Gift of the Wolf

"YOU'RE NOT GOING OUT IN THIS, ARE YOU?" Shaun asked, parting the drapes and peering through the streaky windowpanes at the leaden clouds spitting drizzle towards the already sodden ground. "You don't have to be a genius to know it's going to pour. With your lungs, you're likely to catch pneumonia."

I pulled up the zipper on my waterproof jacket and plonked a cap on my head. "It's our final day here. If I don't see it now, I never will."

"Lot of fuss to make over an old rock."

"It's not a rock. It's a sculpted stone. The Beast of Rannoch Moor."

"Some beast," Shawn grumbled as he reached for his own jacket. "But I'd best come along. Just to make sure you don't get lost."

I grinned and collected my camera while Shaun searched for and found the keys to the rental car. He didn't mind driving on the left; I wasn't about to risk life or sanity.

The clouds appeared lower and denser outside than they had from the warmth and security of the bed-and-breakfast cottage where we had stayed the past two nights. I had to admit to myself that Shaun had a point—it wasn't the best day to be tramping about on a bleak, windswept moor. But inclement weather wasn't going to deter me.

After traversing several miles of paved road, Shaun turned off on a farm track, proceeded a short way, then pulled the car over to the side and parked.

"Let's have at it," he said glumly, and we climbed out.

I pointed to a faint trail running out into a wilderness.

"This way," I said, glad for the directions we'd extracted from the farmer whose land adjoined the moor.

I glanced towards the dilapidated farmhouse that stood dejectedly at the entrance of the lane. Yesterday, I had knocked nervously on the front door.

"'Tis not the place you want to go, lass," said the dour old farmer who'd opened the door, stepped out into the afternoon, and listened to my stammered query.

"Why not?" I'd asked.

"It's not healthy." His dour expression intensified. "It's said as how those that visit the stone are never the same."

"See," Shaun had said from behind me.

"Not the same, how?" I'd asked, ignoring Shaun.

"Can't say for certain." The farmer scratched his head.

"Morphed into werewolves, no doubt," Shaun muttered.

"Eh? What's that?" the farmer demanded.

"Nothing," I said, giving Shaun a dirty look. "He's getting his legends mixed up. Wulvers," I added pointedly to Shaun, "were said to inhabit the Shetland Islands, not the Highlands."

The farmer raised muscled shoulders in an exaggerated shrug. "Don't ken as to what you're talking aboot. But do as you wish, lass. I'm just telling you that it's not wise to have aught to do with druid stones."

"I'll be careful."

"Follow the trail across the lane," he said as he retreated inside. "You'll come across it eventually."

I'd had to restrain myself from laughing. Only when safely back in the car had I allowed myself the luxury.

Druid stones indeed!

But the old farmer's words came back to me as we sloshed

along the trail, glad of our wellies, and I felt the merest tingle of apprehension.

Once on the moor, with no trees to blunt its edge, the chill wind whipped across the exposed flesh of our faces. The trail became harder to follow as it wound around rocks, across bogs, and beside dismal pools. Obviously, only a very few people had trekked out to the stone.

We saw no one—the moor deserted but for a few soggy sheep with splotches of blue paint on their flanks.

In the distance, the Black Mountain, ringed by cloud and gloomy in the half-light, crouched on the horizon like a mythical creature. What else might be lurking in this wasteland? I wondered, shivering, despite my heavy woolen sweater, as rain seeped through my supposedly impermeable jacket. No wonder that Scotland was filled with tales of wraiths and kelpies and bogles and goodness only knew what other creatures—

"Aagh!"

I whirled around at a sudden exclamation and splash from behind me.

Shaun was hauling himself from a particularly large and mucky puddle, a pained expression on his face.

"What's the matter?" I asked, hurrying to give him a hand.

"Slipped on a rock," he replied, grimacing as he stood up. "Twisted my ankle."

"Broken?" I asked as he gingerly put weight on it.

"I don't think so. Probably just a sprain. Look, why don't you go and see your rock—"

"Sculpted stone."

"—while I make my way back to the car."

"Sure you can make it?" I asked. "I could give you a hand—"

"I'll be fine." He motioned towards the clouds, which looked heavier than before. "Go on before it really begins to pour."

"All right."

Shaun turned and, dripping mud, began to limp back the way we had come.

I pressed on into the gloominess of the moor, scanning every shadow, every irregularity in the terrain for the stone.

It had nothing to do with the Neolithic peoples who erected so many standing stones and stone circles. Neither was there any relation to the Druids. It was, rather, Pictish, created by those ancient inhabitants who intermarried with the Gaelic Scotti to become the ancestors of the modern Scots.

Christianized by St. Columba in the sixth century, the Picts had dotted the countryside with carved stones, some bearing religious symbols, other inscribed with more enigmatic markings. I had marveled at the Knocknagael Boar stone in Inverness, which had whetted my appetite to see the Beast of Rannoch. Archaeologists had debated what the carving represented, but to my mind it was easy—it was a wolf. The Rannoch Wolf Stone, I called it.

And why not?

Wolves had thrived in Scotland until, according to unsubstantiated legend, the last one was slain by a giant of a man named MacQueen in 1743 near the River Findhorn, not far from Inverness. And, given the wolf's almost mystical stature among many of the world's cultures, it would have been unusual if the Picts had not respected and emulated this creature, showing their reverence by recording its image in stone. Let the experts argue among themselves. I was convinced.

And so, in this now wolfless landscape, I was desperate to see for myself this enduring record of a lost time, to listen for the echoes of what had once been.

Shaun had never understood my fascination with wolves. To him, they were the marauding demons of legend, devourers of flocks and children. To me, they represented something else entirely.

I slogged on for perhaps a mile, becoming colder and wetter and more miserable with every step.

The moor, I supposed, looked much the same as it had centuries ago when wolves roamed Scotland—small lochs interspersed with bogs and stretches of heather-clad rocky hummocks. But, as for the rest of Scotland, without wolves to control them, the deer had multiplied unrestrained. Unwilling to coexist, humans had wrested the crown of top predator from the wolves, but we were no match for them in terms of managing the ecosystem, and the result was denuded hillsides and glens.

Without wolves, everything became out of sync, like an orchestra lacking a conductor. Similar ecological disasters had occurred in Yellowstone, Italy, and perhaps elsewhere.

All because the wolf had fallen prey not only to men and guns but to exaggerated stories and dark myths. Reviled, cursed, exterminated.

I plodded on.

And then I saw it.

A slab of gray stone perhaps four feet tall sticking out of the ground at a wonky angle.

I covered the last few yards in a dash and heedless of the mud, dropped to my knees in front of it.

With my finger, I traced the eroded image my eyes made out.

The pictures I'd seen hadn't done it justice. Surely it was a wolf. There were the erect ears, the powerful body, the bushy tail, the long muzzle with sharp canine teeth, and the eyes . . .

The eyes.

They were red, glowing . . .

No. They were amber, almost golden, and they were gazing at me.

Gazing not fiercely or hungrily, but with intelligence and curiosity, compelling—no, commanding—my attention.

It was a stone, my reason told me. Gneiss or something. The eyes couldn't be amber...

But they were, my own vision insisted, and ringed by black and surrounded by folds and waves of russet, tan, and gray.

I don't know why, but some inner compulsion urged me to lean forwards, and I rested my head against the stone, cheek to muzzle, expecting to feel the coldness of rough, wet rock.

Instead, I felt softness and warmth. And before I could yank my cheek away, no longer was I kneeling on a muddy, rain- and windswept moor. I was running easily, effortlessly over it, as if I were mistress of my world. Running, with both freedom and terror. For behind me lay fear—and sudden loud noises and acrid smells, and the shouts of men and the baying of monstrous hounds, and my packmates weltering in their own blood. Ahead lay uncertainty and the trepidation that, no matter where I ran, I would find myself alone in this vast landscape.

Eventually, the sounds of pursuit faded and vanished. The rain stopped and, high overhead, the full moon peeked from between wispy clouds, shedding pale light over the hills and the heather, and I was no more than a fragment of moonshadow cast over the landscape. I tipped back my head and howled and waited for an answer, but there was none.

Part of me knew that men were afraid of wolf-howl, that eerie sound which brought a shudder to the nerves and a chill to the blood and raised the hairs on the back of the neck. And yet it was no more than wolf-talk. For wolves, when they hunt, hunt in silence.

I ran on, scenting for spoor, and finding none.

At last I tired and, finding a rocky alcove, curled up and slept.

Morning dawned, and I resumed my quest. The sun shone, and I ran through purple heather and besides lochs that shone blue under a cloud-dotted sky. Mile after barren mile sped beneath me; I saw many deer, and a skittish fox crossed my path, but of my own kind there was not a trace. Once the scent of man reached me, faintly on the breeze, and I gave it a wide berth.

Loneliness gripped me, especially when a pair of golden eagles soared high overhead.

I reached the Black Wood, and surely there among the old pines I would find one of my own. But though I scented wildcats and small mammals—many creatures that made way for me, for who would hinder a wolf?—there was no wolf-scent. I followed trail after trail through the fragrant woods, but disappointment dogged my every step.

At last I chanced upon a small cave—cool and dry and perfect for a den—but, again, devoid of scent.

Weary and disheartened, I lay down to sleep.

In the morning, snow had fallen, a glistening white blanket draped over trees and the undulating moor beyond. I ranged far and wide, but no wolf-tracks save my own disturbed that whiteness and, yet again, no reply came to my yearning howl, and eventually I returned to the cave.

Too dispirited even to hunt, with tail over nose, I waited for the final sleep. And I dreamed of the days when I ranged freely through the glens and over the mountains; I tasted the thrill of the hunt and the warm deer-flesh that enabled my pack and me to survive; I remembered the comfort and security of the den and the wriggling pups seeking milk; yet lurking underneath all this was the dread of the ancient foe that hunted wolfkind mercilessly.

I became conscious of a presence beside me and, in a flash, I whirled around, trying in one motion to see what threatened me and seeking for a way of escape—

"Alana! Alana!"

A strong force grabbed my shoulders and shook me, and I struggled to free myself—

"Alana! Calm down! Calm down! What's gotten into you? Ouch!"

Something slapped my cheek, hard.

"Alana! It's me!"

Gradually the words penetrated my consciousness. As they did so, a lean, dark shadow slipped past me and disappeared, and I jerked back to awareness to find myself being supported upright. One cheek was numb and raw from where it had rested against the stone, the other tingled. My knees hurt, but not as much as the aching loneliness inside.

"Sh–sh–sh–Shaun?" I stuttered, confused, and torn by a yearning for the freedom of the wild, open spaces and a life without constraints. If only I could tear free—

"Yes," he said, and I tried to focus my eyes on him. As I did so, for a fleeting moment, I didn't see my husband in a black raincoat with the hood pulled up. Instead, I had a bizarre vision of Saint Francis of Assisi, the friend and benefactor of the wolf of Gubbio. A man who had seen not a mindless, ravaging beast but an intelligent living creature with its own needs and right to existence; a man who had brought harmony out of fear and hatred. I wondered where all the Saint Francises of the world had gone to.

"Are you all right?" Shaun asked, releasing me.

"I think so. Just c-cold."

"I'm not surprised. You've been gone for hours. I thought you'd fallen or gotten lost."

Fallen. Suddenly, I remembered.

"Your ankle! How did you—"

"It wasn't easy," he said, and I noticed that he was leaning on a sturdy walking stick. His hair was plastered to his scalp and his face was tired and drawn.

I stretched up to kiss his cheek. "I'm sorry ... I don't know what came over me. I must have fallen asleep. I had the strangest dream."

"About a wolf, no doubt." He cast a jaundiced glance at the stone, at the outline of the wolf.

I half expected to see the eyes glowing, but there was only the color of stone.

"Yes, it was very odd. It was as if—"

"Tell me later," he interrupted. "Let's go home."

"Lean against me," I said, slightly miffed, and we began to make our staggering way back to the car.

As we walked, I listened, hoping to hear the mournful, eerie howl of a wolf. Of the last wolf. Of the wolf of Rannoch Moor.

But there was only the patter of the rain and the keening of the wind.

It wasn't until we were back in the shelter of the car and I unzipped my jacket that I noticed it. A tuft of tan and gray fur caught in the zipper near my neck. I worked it free and held it between my fingers.

"What do you have?" Shaun asked, glancing my way as he put the car into gear, then turned up the heat.

I was asking myself the same question as I studied the strands. Was it a freakish coincidence? A fragment or relic of the past? Then, recollecting how those amber eyes had looked at me with, I realized now, a sense of distant kinship, I said, "It was a gift."

THIRTEEN

An Eddy in Time

AT FIRST, THE PRESENCE OF THE OLD MAN SITTING on the bench perched on the hillside barely registered, my mind preoccupied with details of how I should redecorate the cottage into which I had recently moved. Should I paint—and if so, what color paint?—or go with wallpaper? What style of curtains and design would go best? Which would more practical—carpet or hardwood floors?

It was only as I drew nearer and realized that he was talking to himself, but in such a low tone that I couldn't make out the words, that I paid more attention to him. I slowed my pace, trying to study him without being too obvious about it, although his focus seemed fixed on the fields and hills that spread out in a verdant panorama bisected by the blue thread of a stream.

He looked to be about seventy years old, give or take, with disheveled grey hair that hung limply over the collar of his shirt. His clothes, though worn, were clean—a faded green sweater and tan slacks, a flat cap, and Ipswich Town Football Club scarf. Gnarled fingers played about each other, and his head moved rhythmically up and down.

There really wasn't anything distinguishing about him. And Maggie, my Alsatian, whose morning walk this was, didn't show a flicker of interest in him, more concerned about the activities of a foraging squirrel. Yet, for some inexplicable reason, I felt a hint of curiosity. Especially, now that I came to think of it, because I'd seen him on this same bench several times before.

The squirrel retreated to the safety of a tree and Maggie,

impatient that I had slowed down, tugged me onwards, away from the old man.

When I returned home, I found my neighbor, Allison Finch, working in her garden and asked her who he was. I had quickly learned that Allison, a lifelong resident of the village, knew everyone and everything.

"That would be Tom Rimert," she replied as she set a rose bush in a hole. While she shoveled in soil, then patted it down, she went on. "He's always sitting there on Hobson's Hump, every morning since his wife disappeared."

"Disappeared?" I echoed.

"Must have been fifteen or sixteen years ago." She stood and brushed off her hands. "A long time, anyway. One day she was here, the next she was gone."

"What happened?" I asked.

Allison shook her head. "No one knows, Kate. She just vanished without a trace. The police investigated, of course. At first, they suspected Tom, but there was never any evidence of foul play. They searched everywhere. I think they finally decided she just left."

"For another man?" I wondered, thinking that such occurrences weren't uncommon.

Allison shrugged. "That's the official line. Tom will give you a different one. Fetch that watering can for me, won't you?"

"What's his?" I asked, collecting said can and handing it to her.

"Why don't you ask him yourself?" she replied, drenching the newly planted rosebush. "He's a local fixture, after all. Mind you, he's been a bit dotty ever since she disappeared."

"Maybe I'll do that," I said slowly, mildly miffed that Allison wouldn't tell me herself. Talking to dotty people wasn't really my cup of tea. "I walk that way most mornings with Maggie."

The next day it poured heavily, from morning 'til dusk.

Maggie looked out the window, gave a displeased grunt, and curled up on her mat for the duration. The next day was just as bad, and so a further twenty-four hours passed before we were able to take our customary perambulation.

We passed through the village and climbed the slope, I being careful not to slip on the wet grass. No sense spraining a knee just to satisfy my curiosity. I wondered if he would be there.

He was. I sat down on the other end of the bench, while Maggie ambled off to nose in some bushes. Tom didn't seem to be aware of my presence, and I suddenly found myself at a loss as to what to say. Perhaps a simple introduction . . .

"I'm Kate MacIntosh," I said. "This is Maggie."

At first, I thought he wasn't going to respond. Then, without looking towards me, he said, "You're new to the village."

"Yes," I replied. "I moved here a month ago. From Bristol."

"Family?"

"Just Maggie. My husband died last year."

He gave a grunt, then said, "Hope it suits you here," in a tone that gave the distinct impression that he was disinclined to say more. I figured that was enough for one morning.

"Come, Maggie," I called. "Have a good morning," I said to Tom, and rose.

Dealing with decorators and plumbers occupied the next morning, much to Maggie's displeasure, but the following day found us taking our accustomed walk.

Again, I sat down on the far end of the bench, but this time waited for Tom to open the conversation. When he did, his words surprised me.

"Do you ever wish you could go back to the past?" he asked.

I nodded slowly. "There are things I wish I could do differently, words I wish I could retract. Experiences I'd like to relive . . ."

Like those with Michael before cancer had carried him off,

far too young. I thought of the retirement we'd planned but would never share, our dreams of growing old together dashed...

"But, of course, it's impossible," I concluded.

"That's what they say," Tom commented. "Those scientific chappies."

"Aren't they correct?" From the brief snort with which he responded, it seemed that I had exhausted Tom's fund of conversation for the morning. I began to suspect that our conversations were likely to be short and cryptic. I still wanted to ask about his wife but feared he wouldn't answer. So, I bade him good-day and carried on.

Allison laughed when I told her about the brief visits.

"Tom's always been a man of few words. But now they are even fewer. You're doing well, Kate."

The subsequent day dawned misty, with a gentle white shroud blanketing the hills and reducing the sun to a mere shimmer. Maggie was undeterred, but I put on a warmer jacket. I doubted that it would be a morning to meet Tom. But there he was, in his usual place, overlooking the valley. He was wearing a heavier sweater than usual and had his blue and white Ipswich Town FC scarf wound tightly around his neck.

"It's pretty," I said, "even in the mist."

"Especially then," he countered.

"But you can't see anything," I protested.

"No, girl, that's when you can see the most."

"I don't follow," I said, perplexed.

"It's in the mist that you can see them."

I studied the featureless whiteness. "Them? Them who?"

"Them," he repeated quietly but firmly.

I began to wonder if this was what Allison meant when she said he was a bit dotty.

The mist was chilly. I pulled up the collar of my jacket and headed home.

Affairs of one sort or another kept me busy for several days. When next I saw Tom, it was with the words of a hymn that I had heard on the radio that morning running through my mind.

> *Time like an ever-rolling stream*
> *Bears all its sons away;*
> *They fly forgotten, as a dream*
> *Dies at the opening day.*

I must have been singing the words to myself, for Tom said, "It's like that, isn't it?"

Coming as they did so unexpectedly, the words took me by surprise, and I stood there speechless.

Tom motioned towards the stream flowing through the valley. "A stream that passes by and is gone," he continued. "And each of us is carried daily on our own stream. Do you ever wonder about it?"

I found my voice. "I haven't given it much thought."

"I have. For nearly twenty years."

"That's how long you've been coming here?"

He waved a hand in the direction of the stream. "A river isn't regular, is it? There are swirls, eddies ... sometimes the water circles around, coming back to where it started ... around and around ..."

"I suppose you're right," I said.

"Suppose?" he exclaimed, turning to face me. "Of course, I am. Just use your eyes."

His were a piercing blue, reminding me uncomfortably of a very demanding professor I had once had the misfortune to study under.

I squirmed. "Is—is time like that, do you think?"

"Mostly it floats downstream and is lost to us, but every now and then—just occasionally—it comes back around again. And if someone sees it ... well, they think they've seen a ghost. But really, they've just glimpsed an image of the past. Do you believe in ghosts?"

The question caught me off guard. "I'm ... I'm not sure."

He raised white, Einstein-like eyebrows.

"I mean ... I've never seen one. But I've met people who say they have." I almost hesitated to ask. "Have you?"

I was expecting a simple "yes" or "no," but instead he said, "If people are charitable, they think I'm a harmless eccentric pining for a wife who deserted him. If not so charitable, then mentally deranged. Delusional."

I didn't know how to reply to this.

Fortunately, he didn't seem to expect me to, and after a few moments of silence, I took my leave.

And I was hesitant to approach Tom again, although I dearly wanted to hear his version of his wife's fate. Had she really deserted him for another man? Had she wandered off in an amnestic state? Could he have murdered her and hidden her body somewhere—perhaps in the valley below?

Allison laughed when I broached the idea to her. "Tom wouldn't hurt a fly."

"But a wife isn't a fly," I countered.

"Besides, the police investigated that angle."

"They're far from infallible."

"I still can't imagine it."

I could, but perhaps I read too many mystery novels, and Allison knew Tom far better than I.

The leaves began to fall, and autumn was on its way. Would Tom keep his vigil through the winter? I hoped it wouldn't take that long to pry an answer from him.

"There was a settlement down there, you know. Saxon," he said on another misty morning, when the distant trees were faintly visible like a massed army across the stream. "The archaeology chaps deny it. But I know it was there. I've seen it."

"Seen a picture, like an artist's reconstruction?" I ventured.

He shook his head angrily. "Seen it," he repeated forcefully.

"Like one of your eddies in time?" I asked.

He nodded vigorously. "Yes. And that's where she went."

It took a moment for to words to register. "Your wife?"

"Angela. Yes. She always loved anything to do with the past."

"But, the police..."

He made a dismissive gesture. "The coppers think she scarpered with another bloke. But I know she went down there."

He had a walking stick with him today and pointed with it into the valley.

"Into the past?" I goggled. "Are you saying that she's living in some ancient Saxon village?"

"Exactly." He cracked a grin. His teeth were white. "That's why everyone thinks I'm nutters."

And that's what I thought, too.

"But why would she?" I exclaimed.

"Just curious, I expect. She could never resist if she saw something interesting."

"But what about the language?" I persisted, trying to counter his delusion. "It's not as though they spoke modern English. She wouldn't be able to understand a word!"

He shrugged. "She'd manage. Always good at picking up lingo, she was."

I gave up.

Trees in the mist. A fixed delusion. It wouldn't take much for a person to imagine seeing something.

Later, I relayed this to Allison.

"I told you," she replied. "But I'm glad you were able to find out for yourself."

"I feel sorry for him. Sitting there day after day, looking for something that doesn't exist."

"There are worse things."

"I suppose. Has anybody tried to talk him out of it?"

"Of course. But he won't take meds, and since he's harm-less..."

How true.

I decided the best thing was just to be friendly to Tom and leave him in his imaginary world.

I was laid up for a week or so with a cold and, when I saw Tom again, he seemed more distracted than usual, tracing circles on the ground with the tip of his walking stick.

"It must come around again," he muttered. "It must." He stared at me.

"When ... when was the last time you saw ... whatever?" I asked awkwardly.

"Ten years ago," he replied promptly. "But I didn't realize ... I was too slow."

I gazed down the slope of the hillside. Perhaps I lacked imagination but, for the life of me, I couldn't picture anything there.

"But you never know," Tom mumbled, his voice full of sadness. "You just never know. Sometimes people see things for a while ... and then never again."

I wanted to put my arm around his shoulders but didn't think he'd appreciate the gesture.

Maggie wasn't so restrained, leaning against his leg. He patted her head absently.

Instead, I walked home slowly. It was all too bizarre. What, I wondered, was it like for people stuck in an eddy of time—if such a thing even existed? Did they ever die? Did they keep reliving the same things over and over again? Did time flow backward and then forward again? It made no sense.

Perhaps it was all Tom's defense mechanism against the loss of his wife—so he would have some hope to cling to, some way to avoid facing the pain of loss. That, I could understand. I would have given anything to have glimpsed Michael again, to be assured that he was in a better place. But he had died in the sterile environment of a hospital, while receiving the last rites. I had no sight to walk by, only faith, which some days felt as insubstantial as the mist.

Maybe Tom needed the comfort of a priest. I decided to bring that up the next time I saw him.

But on the morrow, Tom wasn't there. It was a damp, chilly morning, with strands of mist writhing between the distant trees. Just the type of morning to encourage a vivid imagination to see ghosts or phantasms of the past. Well, Tom was old. Perhaps he hadn't felt like venturing out.

But the next day, he wasn't there, either.

Worried, I consulted Allison.

"Ask the police to go around to his house," she suggested.

I did, and Maggie and I accompanied a young constable to Tom's cottage at the other end of the village.

"He's probably just laid up with the gout, or something," the constable said, as he knocked on the door.

There was no answer, and after a minute, the policeman tried the knob. The door swung open.

"Mr. Rimert!" he called. "Are you home?"

There was no reply.

I followed him inside, and we checked all the rooms of the modest abode. There was no sign of Tom.

"His wellies are gone," I said, pointing to a couple of muddy patches near the door where boots had probably stood. "And his walking stick."

"He probably just wandered off," the constable said. "Old folks do that sometimes. I'll file a report and we'll keep our eyes open for him, but he'll turn up again, you'll see."

He departed, and I thought I'd check the bench on Hobson's Hump, just in case.

But when I arrived, the bench was unoccupied. I sat down and let my gaze wander over the hillside to the willow-fringed stream and the forest on the farther bank. Tom's scarf should be easily visible against the autumn background, but I saw no hint of blue.

Maggie had been nosing in the grass, some ways down. She straightened up, trotted back to me with her tail up, and nudged my leg. I held out my hand.

"What did you find, girl?"

She dropped a coin onto my palm. Picking up coins was a trick I had taught her long ago.

"Somebody dropped a pound?" I wondered. "Good find, Maggie."

I was about to deposit it in my pocket, but it didn't feel like a pound coin. I looked at it more closely.

It wasn't a pound. It was something you'd find in a museum, or that a treasure hunter with a metal detector might discover in a field.

Worn lettering coursed around the rim—I made out the word 'rex' but could make no sense out of the rest. In the center was what appeared to be the head of an armed man. On the reverse was a cross and an abstract design.

I gazed out over the fields and hedgerows, to where a Saxon village might—despite the opinion of experts—once have stood.

Most likely the constable was right and Tom Rimert would turn up in a few days.

But somehow, I didn't think he would.

And in my heart, I hoped not—that instead, he had found Angela again.

FOURTEEN
The Priory

THE DREAM BEGAN AS IT ALWAYS DID, WITH A vague, diffuse lightening that reminded him of the first, hesitant premonition of dawn. And yet it was subtly different from the sunrises he observed from the back garden of his cottage, when the rising sun scaled the crests of the hills and launched into the sky. Had he been an artist, he might have painted it as a background to a scene on an alien planet, so unearthly was the impression it made upon his sleeping mind.

And though there was nothing of substance to be seen, he felt a sensation of solidity, as if the fading darkness had concealed something—a something that was ready to emerge from the curiously colored haze.

And emerge it would. It always did.

"IS THIS REALLY the sort of place to bring a dying man?" Benjamin Rushmore asked, as the car came to a halt in a narrow layby. He peered out of the passenger side window of his wife's Vauxhall. As on so many country lanes, a tall hedgerow backed by a strand of beech trees paralleled the course of the road, making it impossible to see over from his low vantage point.

"It's good for you to get out of the house," replied his wife Rayna, turning off the engine and opening her own door.

"Good, how?"

"Fresh air," she replied, climbing out and coming around to his side of the car.

"My lungs are fine," he said, as she opened his door, something he lacked the strength to do. "It's only the rest of me that's shot."

"For exercise, then."

"Won't do me any good," Benjamin grumbled as he grasped her hand and allowed her to help him to his feet, where he stood shakily, leaning against the car for support. At first, in the early days after his diagnosis, he'd refused help, determined to maintain his mobility and independence, but those days had passed. Now, resigned to the rapidly approaching inevitable, he accepted the help he knew he needed. "More ruins, I suppose," he continued, taking a firm hold on his walking stick. "Is it right to drag a ruined man to a heap of ruins?"

"You are not a ruin," Rayna countered sharply, wrapping a scarf around his neck. "You mustn't talk like that."

He mustered a slight shrug as he took a first tentative step. "Drape a cape on me and I'd be Superman," he said sarcastically.

"Just come along," she urged.

"All right. But not too quickly. And not too far."

Becky meant well, he knew. But, truth to tell, he came on these little expeditions for her, because it gave her a sense that she was helping him, when, in fact, there was no helping to be done.

She steered him to an opening in the hedgerow. Beyond it, across a strip of field, lay a small grove of trees.

She pointed. "Just behind them."

He took a deep breath. "I think I can manage that."

SLOWLY, THE HAZE assumed more defined colors— although they were difficult to put names to—and a shape emerged. At first it was nothing but an amorphous darker patch silhouetted against a yellow-and-mauve-like sky. But gradually details emerged, and he discerned a rounded, doorless entry set in a crumbling stone wall. Above it were the jagged remnants of a circular window, in which no glass remained. And on either side of the structure stood a pair of skeletal trees, their limbs like twisted and broken arms.

Closer still, leaning at various angles, was a scattering of weathered tombstones, their inscriptions unreadable.

Tombstones.

Always the tombstones.

IT WAS A sunny day, late in the spring, with a fragrance-laden breeze whose coolness belied the coming summer. Once he would have reveled in such a glorious day—and he hadn't even expected to survive the winter to see spring again—but now he had simply to concentrate on remaining upright. He had nothing to spare to appreciate the sheep-dotted countryside bursting with the verdant green of new growth.

Despite being well-worn, the path was uneven, and it wasn't easy to traverse even the short distance across the field, not with his legs feeling like they wouldn't support a mouse and his balance as unsteady as the one and only time he'd overindulged as a teenager. It was hardly surprising, though, as he'd reached the point where he could barely eat or drink. A feeding tube? No thank you. But, with Rayna on one side and his walking stick on the other, he made it and finally stood panting at the edge of the trees.

She said nothing, giving him a minute to catch his breath.

"I'm ready," he said at last, and together they made their way through the trees.

They stepped out into a clearing, and Benjamin halted with an exclamation of surprise.

"What is it?" Rayna wondered.

"I've been here before," Benjamin said, his voice hoarse.

"You never told me!" Rayna exclaimed.

"I never knew," he replied.

IT HAD BEGUN innocuously enough, but by then, although he didn't know it, it was already too late.

A faint yellowing of the whites of his eyes, that was all. He put it down to fatigue. And then his skin appeared more yellow than usual. Too many carrots, he thought, vowing regretfully to cut back on his consumption. And when his urine became an ugly brown? Obviously dehydration. He determined to drink more water.

But then Rayna returned from a week-long skiing trip in Switzerland. He'd met her at the airport.

"Benjamin!" she'd exclaimed, her excited expression changing rapidly to one of shock. "What's the matter with you?"

"Nothing much, I expect," he'd replied.

"Have you seen a doctor?"

"No."

"You're going to, right away."

He'd known better than to protest.

A few blood tests, a CT scan, and he had his diagnosis, given to him by his glum-looking physician.

Metastatic pancreatic cancer.

Palliative surgery might help with some of the symptoms. He could try chemotherapy, but the odds of success were vanishingly small.

In other words, he was going to die.

And it wasn't going to be long. Six months at the most, if he was lucky.

A CHURCH. A long-abandoned church, now nothing more than ruins, the majority of the stones removed for other purposes—to build walls or homes or barns. He guessed it might date from the twelfth or thirteenth century, although he knew little about church architecture and his guess might be wildly stray of the mark. The tombstones, he supposed, were later additions.

And now that he could view the structure and, although he couldn't see anyone, he had the distinct sensation that he wasn't alone.

"YOU NEVER KNEW that you'd been here before?" Rayna frowned. "That makes no sense."

Benjamin noticed a wooden bench, made his way over to it, and lowered himself down.

"I remember it from childhood," he said. "My parents brought me when I was seven or eight years old. But I never learned the name of the place, or where it was located."

"Ashbrook Priory," Rayna said, moving a few feet away to read a descriptive sign. "It was a Benedictine house that flourished until the Dissolution of the Monasteries by Henry VIII."

"It has hardly changed," Benjamin said, studying the gaunt outline of the surviving wall with its fragmentary rose window. "Except that the trees were alive." He indicated the two skeletal trees that framed the remains. "Of course, I remember it as being larger."

Rayna strolled over to the doorway. "Come and look inside," she called.

Benjamin shook his head. "No thanks."

She disappeared through the doorway. Her disembodied voice reached him. "There are several monuments and tombs. Not much left, otherwise."

Benjamin sat with his hands folded in his lap until she returned a few minutes later.

She sat down beside him.

"Thank you for bringing me here," he said. "It's strange the things that can affect a young mind. Don't ask me why, but I have dreamed about this place many times. I even thought about trying to find it, but by then my parents had died and I was living down in Cornwall, and so I never did."

She took and squeezed his hand.

"It was odd," he continued. "The time I was here, I ran ahead of my parents—you know how children do. And as I came through the grove, I was certain there were people here—I think three, and another one passing through the doorway. I believe I was startled rather than scared, but I turned around and ran back to my parents.

"When they reached the priory, though, there was no sign of anyone there. My parents laughed, saying I must have imagined them."

"What were they like," Rayna asked curiously, "the people you saw?"

"I only glimpsed them for a second," Benjamin said, "but I had the impression that they wore black robes with cowls and carried staffs. All except the one entering the church, who held a cross."

"Monks?" Rayna wondered.

"Possibly."

"Do you think you saw ghosts?"

Benjamin stared into the past. "I've wondered about that."

HE SENSED, rather than saw, their presence behind him. There were three and, somehow, he knew they had accompanied him here and felt reassured by their company.

He was glad he wasn't alone, although he knew that this was as far as they could go with him.

He looked up at the sound of a harsh cawing to see a raven perched on the tip of the masonry, above the fractured rose window. A symbol of Saint Benedict, he recalled.

The figures stood motionless and silent behind him.

And then, through the opening of the church, he glimpsed a golden aura.

"I HAD ONCE thought to become a priest, you know," Benjamin added. "Back when I was young and idealistic. It turned out to be only a passing fancy. Instead, I turned away . . . and, worse than that, turned my back on the Church."

"I recall you telling me that," Rayna replied. "For myself, I'm rather glad you didn't join the priesthood."

He managed a thin, rueful smile; raised a withered, yellow hand. "Perhaps you would have been spared this."

"Nonsense! For better or worse, remember?" she said, taking his hand and kissing it. "In sickness or in health."

"Sickness seems to have won," Benjamin said.

"Only temporarily. Not in the end."

"Your faith has always been stronger than mine. Maybe you should have been a nun."

"Me? A nun?" she laughed. "That would have been a riot."

He looked away. "It's fitting, isn't it, that you chose this place for my final outing." He grimaced. "Ashbrook Priory is rather like me. Nothing but an empty shell."

"The material fabric of the building may be gone," she answered, "but the spirit remains. Can't you feel it? And your body may be failing, but you have a beautiful spirit. You didn't become a priest, but you have lived a rewarding life. Many people owe their lives to you."

"Because I managed a charity?"

"Because you showed charity in action."

"Let's not get started with the eulogy," he snorted. "Face it, Becky, I could have done so much more. What a fool I was!"

"Foolish or not, God used you."

"You've got a reply for everything," he said, patting her knee. "No matter what I say—"

"Sometimes, Benjamin Rushmore," she interrupted, but with a twinkle in her eyes, "you really annoy me."

"But not as much as I annoyed Father Davidson," he chuckled, "with my endless questions."

"You got the answers you were seeking," Rayna said. "That's what's important. I'm so glad you decided to come back."

"Better late than never, I suppose."

She put her arm around his shoulders. "Much better."

HE STEPPED FORWARDS, and as he did so, the church sprang into sharper focus. He saw the IHS carved in a roundel to the left of the door, and alpha and omega symbols enclosed in another one to the right.

He'd expected to see fallen masonry, the stumps of walls, perhaps some tombs or monuments, but all was lost in a golden glow.

One more step would carry him across the threshold, but yet he hesitated.

"DEPEND UPON IT, sir, when a man knows he is to be hanged in a fortnight, it concentrates his mind wonderfully," Benjamin said after a pause to gather himself together again, wondering why he was feeling somewhat woozy. And nauseated. He should have tried to drink more at breakfast. "One of Samuel Johnson's witticisms. But it's very true."

"Whatever it takes, I suppose," Rayna sighed. "Still ..."

"My own fault," Benjamin said. "Nobody but myself to blame for being hard-headed."

He shivered, and then the wooziness became weakness and spread over him. Everything began to appear blurry. He tried to raise his hand to his eyes, but it wouldn't move.

"I'm not feeling so well, Becky," he said, as the strength drained out of him. He'd had similar, but milder, episodes before, but this time was worse. Much, much worse. "Perhaps you'd best take me home. Let me lie down."

Concern filled her eyes. "This was a bad idea. I've overdone you."

"No, it was a good idea," he said, as Rayna's face dissolved into a fuzzy ball and started to rotate. Then the world began to slip away and he felt himself sliding off the bench and was powerless to stop himself.

He expected to hit the ground hard, but instead was gently lowered.

He tried to say, "I love you," but wasn't sure if the words came out.

From a distance, he heard Rayna calling for an ambulance.

Then a raven croaked, and he drifted off into blackness.

THE THREE FIGURES were still behind him. Usually, this was where the dream ended and he'd wake up. But this time his dream-self took that final step across the threshold of the church and into the golden glow.

It burned.

It burned as if he was being drenched in liquid fire.

And, strangely, he saw himself as from the outside—as something dark and misshapen, and he recoiled in horror.

But as the fire burned, he saw—and felt—himself transforming. Tthe blackness sloughed off, and something white and shining emerged. He watched, transfixed, as the whiteness spread down his body. But it wasn't his body. It was himself—his soul—his inner being.

Then, feeling as light as light itself, he felt himself rising into the golden glow, and towards a Cross that shimmered in the distance.

THREE PEOPLE STOOD beside the hospital bed.

The priest cleared his throat. "Go forth, Christian soul, from this world, in the name of God, the almighty Father who created you, in the name of Jesus Christ, Son of the Living God, who suffered for you, in the name of the Holy Spirit, who was poured out for you, go forth, faithful Christian. May you live in peace this day, may your home be with God in Zion, with Mary, the virgin Mother of God, with Joseph, and all the angels and saints..."

Rayna gripped the bedrails as the last, weak breaths faltered and stopped, and the wasted form was still.

The doctor listened to the sunken chest with his stethoscope and shook his head.

She leaned forward to plant a final kiss on the cooling cheek.

"Eternal rest grant unto him, O Lord," said the priest, "and let light perpetual shine upon him."

He traced the sign of the cross on the forehead. The doctor pulled a sheet over the peaceful-appearing face.

"It was a severe grace," the priest commented, puffing out his cheeks. "Cancer."

"But in the end, a merciful one," Rayna replied, holding a handkerchief to her eyes, grief, and gratitude mingled. "And necessary."

About the Author

Born in Leicester, England, Andrew M. Seddon enjoys writing in the fields of historical-, science-, and supernatural fiction. When not writing, he enjoys hiking, traveling, and running marathons. He lives with his wife Olivia, German Shepherd Rex, and an assortment of other creatures in Montana and Florida.

DID YOU ENJOY THESE STORIES? Please leave a review on Amazon to help other readers who might like this book. Just a sentence or two saying what you liked will be a big help. And *turn the page for more ghostly tales!*

MORE GHOSTLY TALES
by Andrew M. Seddon

Tales from the Brackenwood Ghost Club

Traditional ghost stories with a Catholic flavor.

Mysterious lights in a buried church...

A half-glimpsed figure haunting a Montana ranch...

An invisible stalker on a California trail...

A shadowy priest who onlly appears on Good Friday...

Welcome to the world of the Brackenwood Ghost Club, whose members meet to hear tales of the strange turnings beyond the world we know.

What Darkness Remains

Thirteen tales of the supernatural and unknown

Alien skulls in the Vatican.

A mysterious monolith on a remote plateau.

Dreaded hounds from another dimension.

A piano piece that should never be played.

A strange door that might—or might not—exist and what lurks behind it.

And eight other tales, not just for the cold, dark nights of winter, but for the days when all seems right with the world...

Made in the USA
Columbia, SC
17 October 2022

69539788R00107